"*I* still say Lord Heathbury is no different from other men," said Lavinia.

Lord Cheriton cupped her chin in one hand and gazed into her face. "My dear Lavinia, you who can flutter your eyelashes at any man and enslave him, a single glance could not dent the heart of this cousin of mine. He is totally immune to feminine wiles."

She tucked her arm into his, looking up at him challengingly. "You are as ever a tease, Cheriton. Of course I can make him interested in me and I promise that you will eat your words before the visit is over. Yes, you will!"

Also by Rachelle Edwards:

DEVIL'S BRIDE   23890 $1.75

WAGER FOR LOVE   50021 $1.75

8999

LORD HEATHBURY'S REVENGE

Rachelle Edwards

FAWCETT COVENTRY • NEW YORK

LORD HEATHBURY'S REVENGE

Published by Fawcett Coventry Books, a unit of CBS
Publications, the Consumer Publishing Division of CBS Inc.
by arrangement with Robert Hale Limited

ISBN: 0-449-50069-1

Printed in the United States of America

First Fawcett Coventry printing: July 1980

10   9   8   7   6   5   4   3   2   1

LORD HEATHBURY'S REVENGE

One

Summer was well-advanced across the English landscape around the country seat of the Duke of Ardsley. Cottonwool clouds scudded across a pale azure sky and groves of oak rippled in the breeze. Beneath the oaks stags and deer browsed, arrogantly conscious of the privilege which allowed them the freedom to roam at will as did the peacocks that strutted on the terraces of Ardsley House.

LORD HEATHBURY'S REVENGE

Only girlish laughter intruded on the peaceful idyll, for although the war against Napoleon waged ferociously on the Continent nothing was allowed to intrude into the round of pleasure sought by all but the poorest of the King's subjects.

A group of women, most of them girls of very tender years, wandered slowly across the fields, chattering happily as they returned from strawberry-picking. All were lightly clad in pastel-coloured muslin gowns, high-waisted and low-necked. Chipstraw bonnets adorned by a variety of ribbons and feathers shielded a dozen fair complexions from the sun and to ward off the danger of a chill most of them wore paisley shawls.

On a divergent course a group of gentlemen returned from an afternoon's successful fishing in the Duke's trout stream. All were men of the *beau monde,* modishly attired even though country living rarely lends itself to the stylishness necessary in Town.

The gentlemen let out a roar of laughter when they caught sight of the girls, brandishing their own catches proudly. In response the girls displayed their baskets, filled to overflowing with ripe strawberries.

Rachelle Edwards

"It is obvious we shall dine on trout and strawberries tonight," declared the prettiest of the girls, Lavinia Merridew, some eighteen years of age, dark-haired with melting brown eyes which invariably caused male hearts to leap.

The Duke's heir, Lord Cheriton, looked at her fondly. "Such are the delights of rusticating, my dear."

"Perhaps we shall all milk the cows on the morrow," she countered.

One of her companions said, affecting an air of boredom, "I confess I much prefer the delights of London."

Lavinia laughed. "Oh, Hattie, we shall *all* be in London before long. And endless round of balls and routs which may become wearying after a while."

"You cannot truly believe that is so."

"No! I am only funning."

"Are you not excited at the prospect of our debut?"

Lavinia's eyes grew round. "Oh yes. Yes indeed."

"I dream every night of the man I will marry," interpolated yet another of the girls, giggling as she caught Lord Cheriton's eye.

9

"You girls talk of nothing else," Lavinia's sister, Mrs Elizabeth Lovell, complained as they approached Ardsley House, outlined against the sky by the setting sun.

"There is nothing else of which to speak," Hattie Durrant declared.

Lord Cheriton, who had been walking alongside them, glanced at Lavinia. "Do *you* dream of the man you will one day marry?"

She grinned engagingly. "Of course. There is not one of us who does not."

A plump girl whose complexion left much to be desired sighed. "It is all very well for Lavinia; she will be the Toast of the Town and receive offers by the score, of that there is no doubt."

Lord Cheriton glanced at Lavinia again. "All the bucks in London may fall in love with Lavinia—as long as she does not become enamoured of one of *them*."

She averted her eyes from his probing gaze, aware of the core of truth in his bantering tone. Having known him all her life like a brother, Lavinia was beginning to realise their relationship would soon be certain to undergo a change, one for which she was not sure she was ready.

"You are a chucklehead, Theo," she retorted to cover up her embarrassment.

"Shall you stand up for a country dance with me at Almacks?" Hattie asked him in a coquettish manner.

"I doubt you would obtain a voucher," he teased and the others laughed.

"What a bore having to partner these chits," cried another of the young blades, and the girls jeered at him.

"Far more interesting to keep company with the Gorgeous Meg or . . ."

He had no opportunity to finish for Mrs Lovell cast him a cold look.

"Who may that be?" Lavinia asked innocently.

The men grinned at each other, ignoring the question which caused Mrs Lovell's lips to draw into a thin line and Kitty Stapleton to giggle behind her hand.

The Duke's Tudor mansion stretched out two wings in welcome and it was to the courtyard the happy party wearily returned.

"Do you go to London when you and your sister leave here?" Hattie asked of Lavinia.

"No, not directly. Elizabeth and I are to accompany Walter—my brother-in-law—

to Bath. He wishes to take the waters."

"It is to be hoped you will allow sufficient time to prepare yourself and buy all the clothes you will need for the Season."

Lavinia laughed. "You can be sure Elizabeth will see we are back in London in good time to do all that is necessary. The London house is being entirely redecorated and I do believe my sister is anticipating my Season with greater relish than I!"

The other girl was wide-eyed. "I cannot conceive why. You are remarkably composed although it is the most exciting happening of our lives. Perhaps," she went on in a confiding tone, "you have already come to an agreement with Someone."

Lavinia found that her cheeks were growing warm, for everyone was aware of the strong bond of affection between Lord Cheriton and herself. However, she replied firmly, "Nothing could be further from the truth. I intend to enjoy myself hugely and have dozens of *beaux*."

"Only think, though," another of the girls broke in excitedly, "the end of the Season will see us all wed!"

"If we are lucky," Hattie murmured.

Kitty Stapleton looked at her askance. "You

may not be, but it is certain Lavinia and I will receive an abundance of offers."

"Oh, you are a beast Kitty Stapleton. With a tongue as sharp as yours it is like to cut a suitor to ribbons!"

"Girls, girls," Mrs Lovell chided. "This bickering is not seemly."

Lavinia linked her arm into her sister's. "It is the excitement and the anticipation, dearest, nothing more."

Mrs Lovell shook her head. "I fear it will all be too much for me. If only Mama were alive."

"I too regret that is not so, but I also know how much you are looking forward to the coming Season. Why else have you prevailed upon dear Walter to provide us both with such gorgeous gowns and jewels?"

"We only wish to launch you in the proper manner, although," she lowered her voice, "I do believe several young men are already in love with you and would need very little encouragement to come up to scratch."

"Well, I am not in love with any of them," Lavinia retorted pertly.

"It will not be long, I'll wager, before we are all cap over the windmill," Kitty added.

Suddenly one of the young men let out a

loud laugh. "Ye gods, Theo, that ancient equipage in the driveway cannot be one of yours!"

Lord Cheriton's eyes narrowed as he looked towards the main porticoed entrance of his father's mansion. Before the wide flight of steps which led up to the entrance stood a truly ancient carriage, shabby and unlike any usually to be seen at Ardsley house where brightly painted phaetons and curricles were more the rule.

The others in the party began to laugh too as Lord Cheriton put one hand to his head. "Oh, he would have to come now of all times."

"Do you mean to say it is not one of *your* carriages, Lord Cheriton," one of the girls teased.

"Naturally not," the young man retorted. "It belongs to my cousin, Heathbury."

Everyone looked interested but it was Lavinia who asked, "I do not recall hearing his name mentioned before. Are we acquainted with him?"

At this Lord Cheriton laughed. "No! He is only lately returned from the Indies, which I must be quick to point out accounts for his . . . strangeness."

14

Before he had any chance to elaborate further a young man appeared at the top of the steps. The moment he saw Lord Cheriton the rather serious cast of his face softened somewhat and he began to hurry down the steps towards him.

The group at the bottom of the steps could only stand and stare at him in astonishment, for his apparel was quite bizarre. In direct contrast to the plain and elegant clothes decreed by Beau Brummel and worn by all who aspired to be fashionable, including Lord Cheriton and his companions, this young man wore the most outmoded apparel; a striped satin waistcoast beneath a flared coat of brown fustian, and breeches buckled at the knee. His fair hair was worn far too long for elegance, heedlessly tied back with a ribbon, and there was too much lace on his carelessly tied neckcloth for the current vogue.

Whilst most of the young men could only stare in astonishment at the figure he presented the girls began to giggle although mercifully the young man seemed unaware of the amusement he was causing.

Mrs Lovell said, "My word," in an amazed tone of voice and Lord Cheriton himself grew red in the face, giving his friends apologetic looks.

"We didn't look to see him here for another sen'night."

"Ah, Heathbury," he said, rallying slightly and clearing his throat, "good to see you again."

"It is good to be back," the young man replied, glancing curiously at last at the others, "but I trust I do not intrude."

Once again Lord Cheriton cleared his throat. "Not at all, dear fellow. Let me introduce our guests. Mrs Lovell, her sister Miss Merridew," this accompanied by a smile. "Miss Stapleton, Miss Durrant, Mrs Whitley, Lords Ratcliffe, Fairfax, Sir Christopher Bonham . . ."

As Lord Cheriton made the introductions, the young man's attention fluttered over them all. Watching with some amusement, Lavinia Merridew suspected that he wasn't much interested or even listening to the introductions.

"The pity is you didn't arrive earlier to join us," Lord Cheriton was saying in a bright voice. "We've had a splendid day's fishing."

"I most certainly would have arrived earlier, only the carriage toppled into a ditch," the young man replied, casting an embarrassed look at the others, "and it took the devil of a time to set it to rights again. A trunkful of books scattered too and had to be retrieved one by one. Then we had gone but a mile further when one of the horses went lame."

"That does not surprise me; those cattle are fit only to pull the plough, and you most certainly need a new carriage, Heathbury. This one was outmoded when your Papa was alive.

"No doubting you're tired after your journey," he went on. "Did you find the house in the devil of a mess when you arrived?"

He put an arm around his cousin's shoulders and began to walk up the steps to the house with him. "I am afraid so," the young man replied. "I made lists of what I deemed necessary to be done in the first instance and must ask Uncle Richard to advise me on the matter."

After giving each other amused and mystified looks, the rest of the party began to follow, many of them questioning amongst themselves who this odd person could be. All of them had known Lord Cheriton since childhood and could scarce credit that they were not also acquainted with his cousin who was not a great deal older.

There was, unfortunately, no opportunity to put to him all the questions they were longing to ask, for Lord Heathbury was still in the marble hall when they reached it. He looked flustered as he darted to and fro, giving garbled instructions to the liveried footmen who scurried here and there, bearing travel-worn trunks which appeared to be heavy in the extreme. His face was growing rather red at the confusion which every word he uttered added. Lavinia and her companions could scarcely laugh out loud, but they were hard put to hide their smirks. Lord Ratcliffe whispered to her as Lord Heathbury accosted first one lackey and then another, "He dances more prettily than any maiden."

Lord Cheriton shrugged his shoulders at them in the most comical manner, and the guests had no choice but to retire to their rooms, their curiosity still unsatisfied.

"Now, Theo, you must tell us where you have been hiding him," Lavinia demanded later that evening. "We are all in a fidge to know."

Looking demure in lilac sarsnet with a

circlet of pearls nestling in her curls, she tended to make all the other females present appear a mite over dressed.

As Lavinia watched him with eyes that sparkled behind her fan, Lord Cheriton glanced across the vast drawing room to where his cousin was seated on a sofa next to an elderly dowager with whom he was in deep and apparently serious conversation. The fact that throughout the evening the young man had eschewed the company of others of a similar age and attached himself to the older members of the company only served to make them even more curious about him. Lavinia had overheard him lecturing one baronet, over dinner, on how Napoleon Bonaparte should be dealt with by the Allies, citing historical precedents by the score when the gentleman in question was only concerned with the scarcity of good brandy.

Now as the evening progressed many of the guests were seated about the room indulging in their passion for whist. Others indulged in faro and hazard whilst some of the ladies took turns to play the harpsichord. Servants mingled with the guests, ensuring that glasses were kept filled, spilled snuffboxes were immediately cleaned away and sconces replenished with candles as the old ones burned low. Despite the various diversions there still remained, however, a number of people anxious to quiz Lord Cheriton about his cousin.

"I don't know what you mean," he answered with maddening nonchalance.

"Why have we never seen him before?" Hattie Durrant demanded. "Has he been hidden away?"

"Of course not," Lord Cheriton answered indignantly. "Why should we do such a thing?"

"The answer to that, my dear fellow," Sir Christopher Bonham answered "should be obvious."

"Is he mad? Has he been locked up in an asylum for years?" Hattie insisted.

Lord Cheriton laughed. "No, you goose! He is as sane as you or I—in his own way, of course."

This remark only served to inflame their curiosity further and knowingly Lavinia remarked, "Lord Cheriton is going to derive as much amusement out of this as he can before we receive our explanation."

"Then we shall just have to stay here until

we have our answers," Lord Fairfax replied, flicking a speck of snuff from the sleeve of his coat. "I am quite convinced that the fellow must have been locked away for ten years to dare appear in public in such a way."

"Not quite so," Lord Cheriton answered and as they glared at him he went on, sighing with resignation, "He is the son of my mother's late brother."

"Why do we not know him?" Kitty Stapleton insisted.

"If you would but allow me to continue," the young man told her, "you will very soon find out."

"Oh do hush, Kitty," Hattie Durrant urged, an edge of excitement to her voice.

"My late uncle, the Earl of Heathbury, as a young man travelled to his extensive estates in the Indies and whilst he was there he met a pretty Creole girl whom he married. He brought his bride back to England where Damien—my cousin—was born. Unfortunately my aunt—although I never met her—could not settle here. The climate was not good for her health and she found the social round a trifle onerous, so the family returned to the plantations.

21

"After my uncle died his wife of course remained where she was happiest but despite every exhortation from my own father she refused to send her son back here to be educated in the usual way. Instead she engaged an English tutor for him, who, to be fair, gave him a better education than he could possibly have received in England." He grinned wickedly. "A classical education, that is, with no diversions. You might discover during the next few days that he has a predilection for Greek philosophers and historians. He reads a good deal of Plato and Aristotle and several others of a similar vein, so unless any of you are familiar with the subject it would be a waste of time to try and engage him in conversation."

"I wouldn't attempt to do so," Lord Fairfax answered, peering at the object of their interest through his quizzing glass.

The girls found this vastly amusing and Lavinia said, "Looking at him I can quite believe all you say, although it is an exceedingly odd tale."

Hattie Durrant squealed with delight. "What a freak. He is not at all like you, Cheriton."

The young man laughed. "I am greatly relieved to hear you say so."

"What prevailed upon Lady Heathbury to allow him to come home at last?" Lavinia asked.

"Nothing ever could. She died last year and it was my cousin himself who decided to come home at last. So, you see, you must all make allowances for his . . . strangeness. Only think on it, apart from his doting Mama, he has had no close companionship save that of an elderly tutor. In fact all his life he has known only blackamoor servants; he has even brought one here as his valet. 'Tis most offputting I confess. I can scarce find a suitable subject on which we can converse."

"No doubt once he is in London that will effect a change," Lavinia prophesised, glancing at him again, "for he is not ill-looking. If his hair was cut in a fashionable manner and with more modish clothes I dare say he would possess quite a pleasing appearance."

Hattie groaned and Lord Cheriton replied, "My cousin has no intention of going up to London. He has declared his intention of renovating his country estates which, in truth are sadly neglected and may take years to put to rights."

"The fellow must be as poor as a church rat," Sir Christopher remarked eyeing the Earl through his quizzing glass.

At this Lord Cheriton threw back his head and laughed. "Would that we were all as poor as he!" All attention returned to the young man who went on, enjoying himself hugely now, "He has several profitable estates in the Indies as well as all the property he has here in England, which even though run down at present are exceedingly profitable. My late uncle was a thrifty man who did not gamble or indulge in any vice that we knew of. There are few enough ways of spending a fortune in the Indies, recall."

They all looked at the young man again—he was quite unaware of the curiosity about him—and it was with renewed interest.

Hattie Durrant twirled a mousy curl around her finger. "No doubt he has come back to select a wife."

Once again Lord Cheriton laughed. "I very much doubt it."

"A fellow of his age and in his position must needs be considering taking one," Sir Christopher remarked.

"Perhaps that fact is apparent to you and to me," Lord Cheriton conceded, "but he is not aware of it at all. Besides," he lowered his voice conspiratorially, "his late Mama would certainly have left him in ignorance of the subtle differences between male and female, apart from the fact that females do not know Latin and Greek."

The young men laughed, but Lavinia looked askance at them. "Cheriton, I declare you do him an injustice!" and they all looked at her once more. She went on, enjoying the audience. "Just because he does not dress as you do and has a serious turn of mind does not indicate that his thoughts and feelings are not as other men's."

Lord Cheriton cupped her chin in one hand and gazed into her face. "My dear Lavinia, you who can flutter your eyelashes at any man and enslave him with a single glance could not dent the heart of this cousin of mine. He is totally immune to feminine wiles."

She snapped her head away from him. "I do not accept that. I still maintain he must enjoy the same weaknesses as his fellow males."

"Hardly," Hattie answered with a giggle.

"Personally I prefer men to be manly."

Sir Christopher was leaning languidly against a marble pillar. He returned his snuff-box to his pocket and said, "There is not even the chance of making the wretched fellow bosky. From what I have observed he is abstemious to a fault."

"You could afford to emulate him," Lavinia countered, still angry at Lord Cheriton's teasing.

"Tut, tut," he answered, his eyes agleam with mischief, "the fair Lavinia's pride has been hurt, Cheriton."

"No such thing was intended for I speak only the truth. He could change if he so wished and I have honestly tried to help him do so but he refuses to be turned into a bang-up blade, or," he added wickedly, "avail himself of female company which I could readily provide for him."

Lavinia turned away, "I still say he is no different to other men."

"I dare say that is true," Lord Cheriton answered with a sigh which indicated his growing boredom with the subject. "In any event I declare it best to leave him to his own devices." He smiled then at Lavinia. "I do believe supper is being served, my dear.

May I take you in?" As she hesitated to take his arm he added, "I promise if you wait for my cousin to approach you, you may wait for ever."

Angry again she tucked her arm into his, looking up at him challengingly. "You are as ever a tease, Cheriton. Of course I can make him interested in me and I promise that you will eat your words before the visit is over. Yes, you will!"

Two

Over the ensuing days, Lavinia observed Lord
Heathbury whenever she was able, for he
was usually absent from the activities orga-
nised to entertain the guests. After several
days she began to acknowledge she would
have to take the initiative in attracting his
interest, for it was plain her natural charm
would not do so.

She learned that he was most often to be
found in the library where he was best able

to study the works of Greek philosophers. As the week advanced and Lord Cheriton gave her knowing smiles each time his cousin passed them with merely an absent nod, she was sorry she had spoken so rashly, and yet she was still determined to win at least a flicker of interest from this boring young sprig.

It was not until several days later that she managed to take breakfast at the same time as he, for it was his habit to rise at an unfashionably early hour, which he could fully afford to do as he rarely caroused into the morning as did the other guests. As she entered the breakfast room on this particular morning she hesitated in order to look around and then smiled brightly, bidding, "Good morning," to all.

Lord Heathbury did not look up, but he half rose from his chair and murmured something incomprehensible before subsiding again. Hattie Durrant and Kitty Stapleton were sitting next to each other and giggling softly behind their hands which spurred on her resolve. Lavinia seated herself near to Lord Fairfax, who had declared himself in love with her, which happened to be opposite her quarry.

"Allow me to fetch you some breakfast, Miss Merridew," Lord Fairfax immediately offered. He too looked mildly amused and Lavinia was beginning to feel exasperated with them all, not the least Lord Heathbury.

Nevertheless, she smiled her thanks and replied, "I should be obliged," although, in truth, she had no fancy for food at that moment.

Lord Fairfax immediately snapped his fingers for the footman to bring fresh coffee and then selected some eggs and kedgeree from silver chafing dishes and placed it in front of her. All around, Lavinia was aware of the great interest centred upon her.

"It was a most pleasant evening yesterday," Lord Fairfax ventured.

"Indeed it was," she answered, making a show of eating and yet surreptitiously eyeing her quarry. "Did you not enjoy it too, Lord Heathbury?"

For a moment the young man paused in his enjoyment of a hearty breakfast and looked surprised. His cheeks deepened in colour before he replied, "My apologies. I was not listening. I . . ."

"Did you not enjoy last night's musical evening?"

"Miss Merridew sings like a lark," Lord Fairfax added. "Would that we could prevail upon her to sing every evening."

The young man's colour deepened even further. "Quite so, Miss . . ."

Lord Fairfax sat back in his chair and looked smug. Lavinia bit back her annoyance at such obvious disinterest and smiled sweetly instead. "Merridew, Lord Heathbury. Miss *Merridew*."

He nodded and returned his attention to his food. When she dared to glance at Lord Fairfax he merely shrugged slightly, but the girls present in the room grinned.

"Lord Heathbury," she persisted, "do you intend to enter the curricle race in the Park this afternoon? It promises to be most diverting."

He looked up again. "I had no notion there was to be one, Miss . . . er Merridew."

"Oh yes indeed, and all must enter." She paused before adding, "All the participants are sporting ladies' colours, just as they did in Medieval jousting tournaments."

"I have no suitable carriage."

He was about to look away again but she persisted, "You could borrow one. Surely you would like to sport the colours of one lady present at Ardsley."

He smiled faintly. "It would be to no avail, Miss Merridew. I do not tool the ribbons well enough, I'm afraid."

Before she had any chance to engage him in further conversation he got to his feet, nodding to all present. "If you will excuse me . . ."

The moment the door had closed behind him to Lavinia's chagrin there arose a howl of laughter which caused the older people present to exhort them to be quiet. Lavinia continued to eat in silence and just as she had finished Hattie Durrant leaned towards her.

"Lord Cheriton and Sir Christopher have a wager between them on who will triumph. I believe the odds are heavily in favour of Lord Heathbury resisting you."

She gave them both a withering look. "My only regret is that one of those chuckleheads will win."

"Oh, admit you have met your match," Kitty urged. "You already have a clutch of *beaux* and the Season is not yet begun. You can surely allow one prosy bore to escape the net."

"I admit to nothing, Kitty. It matters not a jot to me whether the wretched creature spends the rest of his life in love with his miserable old books, but I am certainly not going to spend the rest of mine being teased by Theo Cheriton!"

The great hall of Ardsley House was deserted except for attendant footmen. Lavinia glanced around, however, to ensure she was not being overlooked by any of her friends and then she quietly let herself into the Duke's magnificent library. The Duke of Ardsley had collected a wide variety of tomes as had his father before him, so that the Ardsley collection was now justly famous. The library was a spacious one, double galleried with ample tables and chairs to facilitate those who wished to read there.

Lord Heathbury was seated at one of the library tables and intent upon the book in front of him. Lavinia affected not to have seen him and began to browse along one bookcase.

The scraping of chair legs on the polished floor caused her to look around, her eyes wide with surprise. He had risen to his feet and was looking at her uncertainly.

Rachelle Edwards

"Why, Lord Heathbury, I had no notion anyone was here. I do hope I haven't disturbed you."

He averted his eyes. "Not at all, Miss ... er Merridew."

She smiled. "I was persuaded I was quite alone. I only wished to select a book to while away an hour, so I shall not disturb you for long."

"You need not hurry on my account."

"You're too kind," she beamed and then, "Oh, do be seated, Lord Heathbury. I shall be as quiet as a mouse."

He subsided into the chair again and resumed reading. Slowly she moved along the shelves until she was close to the table.

"Botheration! I seem to be in the wrong section. Would *you* know where the volumes of poetry are kept?"

A flicker of irritation crossed his face as he looked up again. "I believe they are just in front of you, Miss Merridew."

Lavinia laughed. "Oh, what a chucklehead I am. So they are. What a wonderful selection I do declare. Now, shall I read Cowper or Keats perhaps?" She turned on her heel. "As a well-read man, Lord Heathbury, what would you recommend?"

He sat back in the chair and regarded her sombrely. His eyes, she noticed for the first time, were the most incredible shade of deep blue, heightened by his sun-bronzed skin, something to be abhorred in a woman but not unbecoming in a man.

"I am not acquainted with either, Miss Merridew, although I believe they are exceeding well thought of by the masses. My reading has always been of a more serious kind."

Looking intrigued Lavinia seated herself in a chair at the other side of the table. "I envy you that, Lord Heathbury. We females as you may know are not encouraged to read anything of a serious nature, which I believe to be an error."

"I have no opinion on that, Miss Merridew, except to say that those who have no interest in history miss a great deal."

"Oh, I am quite certain you are right in that. Indeed it is a point I was trying to make. I am," she added, "intrigued as to how you came by your extraordinary knowledge in such a far-flung place as the Indies."

He began to look uncomfortable as if he would like to leave but politeness decreed he could not. "I had a most uncommon tutor.

He imparted all his considerable knowledge to me."

Lavinia cupped her dainty chin on her hands and regarded him with a pair of eyes which normally reduced a man to a quivering mass of nerves.

"Tell me what is that book you are reading?"

"Thucydides," he answered in some embarrassment.

"Really? How wonderful of you to be able to understand it. Tell me what it is about."

"I doubt if you would find the subject of interest to you, Miss Merridew."

Coyly she answered, "You have no notion what would interest me, Lord Heathbury."

He drew an almost imperceptible sigh. "The book is the *History of the Peloponnesian War.*"

She sat up straight again and he smiled. "We women," she complained, "miss a deal in our schooling."

"If you are truly interested I believe you would enjoy Aristophanes. His plays are vastly amusing."

She sighed wistfully. "I shall bear that in mind."

"I doubt if you will, Miss Merridew."

Lavinia was certain she detected a hint of amusement in those deep blue eyes and

suddenly felt she might succeed after all.
"Well, I own I shall soon be occupied with
preparations for my Season, which will leave
little time for reading of any kind."

He smiled faintly again. "A most important event, I understand."

"Indeed it is. None more so, but I do feel
that you could teach me so much, Lord
Heathbury."

Once again he looked embarrassed. "I am
certain Mrs. Lovell has schooled you in all a
young lady is supposed to know."

"You are so kind to say so, but you are so
well-read and well-travelled, 'tis truly amazing. I must ensure that my sister sends you
an invitation to my come-out ball."

He closed his book as if conceding he would
not be able to read it now. "That is a most
kind thought, but I regret I shall not be in
London."

Lavinia gasped. "Not in London! Why, Lord
Heathbury, you cannot intend to return to
the Indies so soon."

A ghost of a smile crossed his face. "There
is so much work needed to put to rights my
country estate in Norfolk. I am only just
returned to England and have got to make a
start."

"Theo—Lord Cheriton—did tell me, but that is all the more reason for you to come to Town and enjoy the diversions there before you begin this onerous task."

His eyes narrowed suddenly and Lavinia had the satisfying feeling that he was actually seeing her for the first time.

"You and my cousin have a familiar relationship, have you not?"

She smiled with genuine pleasure at the reminder. "We have known each other all our lives."

Once again he averted his eyes. "You . . . must all find me a trifle . . . odd."

Her eyes were wide with innocence as she replied, "Your notions are a trifle different, which is only to be expected, but that only promotes interest."

"I am not certain I like to be the object of interest, Miss Merridew." Then he hesitated before asking, "When does everyone leave?"

At this Lavinia threw back her head and laughed. "At the end of the week, you will be glad to hear."

Her laughter only served to throw him into some confusion as his cheeks grew pink once more. "As you observe I do not possess a deal of tact."

Lavinia got to her feet at last, ready to concede failure. " 'Tis plain you welcome no company so I shall not distract you any longer, Lord Heathbury. Your patience has been admirable."

She turned on her heel and he said quickly, "Please don't go, Miss Merridew. I confess I am unused to the way of the Society into which I was born. Casual conversation still comes hard to me."

"You are merely out of practice. You have a good deal to say of interest."

"Oh, I was not aware having something to say was necessary to conversation."

Again that hint of humour, but on this occasion it only served to anger her. "We must all seem exceeding foolish to you, Lord Heathbury."

"No. It is I who am foolish I fear. I meant to cause no offence. You see I am ignorant of polite society. There was none to speak of where I have spent the most part of my life. Fortunately after this week is over it will not be necessary."

Lavinia gazed at him, suddenly moved to compassion at that hard won confession. "You could soon learn. Your cousin could introduce you to everyone of his acquaintance and you would soon find yourself in a veritable whirl of activity."

He stared at the floor. "I think not. I wish only to run my estate. The thought of city life holds no lure for me."

"How can that be when you have no notion what it is like? You really should come up for a while. You would enjoy the clubs and riding in the Park. Your cousin goes to mills too, and to the horseracing. Everyone enjoys that."

The young man looked scornful. "Is that all he does?"

"No! The evenings will be filled with a great many balls and routs, visits to Vauxhall and the theatre . . ."

He glanced at her quickly and away again. "My knowledge of dancing is strictly theoretical."

"You would gain practical knowledge soon enough, Lord Heathbury," she said in a mocking tone.

He gave her a challenging look then which she could not fully meet. "Would *you* stand up with me?"

Her face relaxed into a smile at the sight of his uncertainty. "You may be certain I would."

41

His own face also relaxed into the semblance of a smile. "You are too kind, but it remains that I have a deal to do on my estate after a lifetime's neglect."

"If the neglect is so long-standing it will wait another few months. You could still attend to it after enjoying a Season."

"No," he answered firmly. "Whenever I embark upon a course of action, Miss Merridew, I do so with great thoroughness."

Lavinia shook her head with vexation at such surprising stubbornness. Although she had managed to attract his attention and even engage him in conversation it was a far cry from arousing his interest.

"You have led an interesting life . . ." she ventured.

"No, it was not. It was deadly dull."

"Oh, come now, Lord Heathbury," she said in a cajoling tone, "everyone is in a fever to hear about life in the plantations. I am in a fidge to learn what it is like."

"Are you really, Miss Merridew?" he asked eagerly and she was certain at last her patience was going to meet with success.

"Lord Heathbury, I assure you that if you do decide to come to Town you will cause a sensation."

For a moment it appeared that the notion appealed to him, but then he turned away. "Miss Merridew, I will be frank; I wish only to study the Greek historians and philosophers and make my estates even more profitable. Nothing else is of any import to me. I cannot conceive how we became engaged in this ludicrous conversation."

"Nor can I," she answered with a sigh of resignation.

Just as she turned towards the door, however, it opened and Kitty, Hattie and Lord Cheriton came in, halting just inside the doorway in surprise. Of one accord their eyes travelled from Lavinia to the Earl and back again before registering their understanding of her ploy and their amusement. Lavinia looked vexed but affected to be nonchalant.

Grinning knowingly Lord Cheriton said, "Lavinia, we've been scouring the house for you. It is time to leave for our picnic and we have no notion for you to remain behind."

Lavinia made her way purposefully towards the door watched by her friends who could scarce conceal their amusement, but before she reached it she halted and turned around again.

"Lord Heathbury, why do you not join us on the picnic today?"

He looked up slowly from the book to which he had returned and seemed somewhat taken aback.

"I do not believe my cousin will find a picnic in the least diverting," Lord Cheriton answered for him.

"You need do nothing save sit beneath a tree and read," she pointed out, "and I am persuaded the air will do you good. If you insist on remaining indoors your skin will lose that uncommon colour."

"I did manage to study outdoors a great deal in Jamaica," he admitted before snapping the book shut. Once again when he got to his feet, Lavinia noted that he was slightly taller than his cousin and beneath the appalling and ill-fitting coat his shoulders were well-developed. He was not such an ill-looking man after all.

"Don't let Miss Merridew tease you, Heathbury," his cousin said turning away. "Let me tell you she is one of the goose-caps you were decrying to me not long ago." He gave Lavinia a sly glance which caused her to stiffen with indignation.

"On the contrary, Cheriton, our conversation has been most interesting," the Earl contradicted. His eyes met hers briefly. "I

44

think perhaps Miss Merridew is correct; a few hours in the open air may be beneficial."

The two other girls gasped in amazement, Lord Cheriton's face took on an expression of vexation and Lavinia swept out of the room giving them all a look of triumph.

Three

He was painfully shy Lavinia decided. Being
unused to company other than that of his
tutor and his possessive mother he had no
notion how to mix with people of his own
age. The more she observed him, the more
she understood these facts. He could converse
with only those much older than himself.

During that picnic he had seated himself
some distance from the others, leaning against
the trunk of an old oak tree from where he

could observe everything. To Lavinia's disappointment he hardly spoke to her at all, but she had been aware all the while of his questioning gaze, as if he were attempting to solve some mental puzzle about her and the others.

At last she could bear to see him isolated no longer and broke away from her companions, taking with her two dishes of strawberries and fresh clotted cream. Before he could scramble awkwardly to his feet she sank down on the grass nearby.

"I noted you have eaten little, Lord Heathbury. Do you not enjoy picnics either?"

She handed him one of the dishes which he took after exhibiting a little reluctance. "I am not used to them, that is all."

Lavinia ate her strawberries with gusto. "They are the greatest fun. What *did* you do before you came here?"

He began to eat the strawberries at last and it was as if it were an excuse not to look directly at her. "I learned to look after our estates, for my father died when I was very young. Travelling around them was a time-consuming matter. When I was not so employed I studied aspects of history and philosophy which, as you know, are of interest to me."

"Now you are in England you will be able to develop new interests though."

"Oh indeed. I have spoken to tenants on both my uncle's and my own estates and I am most interested in animal husbandry now. The quality of the cattle here is quite astonishing. In fact," he went on, warming to the subject, "I intend to make a study of methods . . ."

Lavinia groaned inwardly but managed to show a coy smile. "But what of your social life, Lord Heathbury? I am persuaded there is a good deal of it in Jamaica."

Once again he averted his eyes, picking absently at a blade of grass. "We had little time to fraternise; plantations are at great distances from each other and many of them are owned by absentee landlords. Of course Mama did know several Creole families who called occasionally."

"No doubt a young man of your standing and address knew a great many young ladies who await your return with much eagerness."

His cheeks coloured, which she knew would

49

happen, and then he looked up saying maddeningly, "Cheriton is beckoning to you, Miss Merridew."

Annoyed, Lavinia looked round to discover that this was so. The other young people were about to make off and she laughed. "He beckons to us both. We are about to engage in a game of hide and seek."

He shook his head. "Oh no. I shall remain here, but do be pleased to go yourself, Miss Merridew."

Lavinia jumped to her feet and stood looking down on him. "I shall certainly do no such thing if you do not. Everyone must participate; I insist upon it." She waved her hand to where everyone was pairing off. "See, you will be quite alone if you remain."

"I am accustomed to it, you know."

"But not when I am around," she answered with genuine compassion. Her task had gone beyond Lord Cheriton's original challenge. She truly did not wish to see him isolated from others of his age. "Lord Heathbury," she insisted, "do you find my companionship so objectionable you cannot bear to partner me?"

Her challenge had the desired effect and he scrambled to his feet. "That is most certainly not true," he protested in outraged tones, "but I am also certain others have a greater claim upon you."

She eyed him with mock severity which caused his lips to curve slightly. "No excuses will weigh with me."

Lord Cheriton came striding up to them. "We cannot begin without you, Lavinia."

"Lord Heathbury is partnering me," she told him, her gaze holding that of the Earl.

Concealing his surprise the other young man answered, "Splendid. Splendid. Come along then." As they began to follow Lord Cheriton paused after a moment to add, "Heathbury, do recall that Miss Merridew is no slave girl and you must observe every propriety even if you find yourselves alone in the woods."

The Earl's cheeks flooded with colour almost to his ears. His step faltered and when it seemed he might cry off after all, Lavinia caught his hand in hers. "Disregard his gammoning, Lord Heathbury," and then laughing gaily she pulled him towards the others.

Lavinia hoped that by persuading him to attend the picnic and participating Lord Cheriton would concede her success, but it was not so as she suspected would be the case although she no longer cared. She was satisfied to have succeeded as well as she had.

It came as no surprise that he did behave towards her with the utmost propriety during the game of hide and seek, disengaging himself from her grasp as soon as was possible and keeping a respectful distance at all times. Their partnership was surprisingly successful for all that, scoring the most wins and fooling everyone when it was their turn to hide.

He watched in amazement as she lifted her skirts, saying, "Help me up into this tree, Lord Heathbury. Quickly before they come to find us!"

"We cannot hide in a *tree*, Miss Merridew."

"Have you never climbed a tree before?" she asked in some astonishment.

"Yes . . . in my youth, and I was soundly thrashed for it."

"You will not be thrashed for it here," she assured him before adding with a grin, "All boys climb trees—some girls too." Then she urged again, "Hurry do. I hear them coming."

"Mrs Lovell would not like this," he warned as he gave her his arm.

"Then it is fortunate she has remained at

the house today," she answered, discovering him to be surprisingly strong.

Despite a proliferation of petticoats and tight seaming in her high-waisted gown, Lavinia succeeded in hiding herself in the oak with her partner clambering up after her.

"You must remember, Lord Heathbury," she told him, "never to breathe a word of our hiding place or I shall not be able to use it again."

"You have my word upon it. I would not for anything spoil your future enjoyment, nor do I wish to receive disapprobation for aiding you in this folly."

"Then it shall be our secret for eternity!"

Her eyes met his and their gaze held for a long moment, causing Lavinia to experience an emotion she could not recognise, before the rustling of the undergrowth heralded the arrival of the searchers.

She watched gleefully as they passed beneath them and when they had gone she gave the Earl a triumphant look whereupon they both broke into peals of laughter, and not for the first time she thought he could be a most personable man if only he would try.

*   *   *

Lavinia felt she would have to be satisfied with the moderate success in drawing him out on that one occasion, however to her delight and Lord Cheriton's chagrin, over the ensuing days it became more and more apparent that Lord Heathbury was becoming rather less interested in his books. More and more he appeared wherever Lavinia happened to be and eventually everyone began to acknowledge it was not a coincidence. He still had little to say, but the way his gaze became simply adoring when it fell upon Lavinia was eloquent enough.

Such a short time ago she would have been delighted to have achieved so hard won a victory but he was such a serious young man it was quite unlike a usual light-hearted flirtation. His devotion was beginning to be an embarrassment. It was rather like having a pet dog in attendance at all times.

Whenever Lavinia was prevailed upon to play the harpsichord it was Lord Heathbury who sprang to his feet in order to turn the pages of her music, or to take her in to supper, and invariably he managed to seat himself at her side at dinner. Although her success gave her a degree of satisfaction it was also tinged with disquiet and she was more than a little relieved when the end of the week approached. Before long she would be *en route* for Bath with Elizabeth and Walter, and Lord Heathbury would disappear for ever to his Norfolk estate to devote his time to animal husbandry. It was also a relief to her that he had not voiced his adoration in words. That, she felt, would be difficult to counter diplomatically.

"Thanks to you, fair Lavinia," Sir Christopher Bonham told her two days before the house party was due to end when he accosted her in the hall, "I am one hundred guineas the richer than when I came."

She was taken aback by this admission. "I cannot conceive why, Sir Christopher."

"The wager. Do you not recall?"

She sighed. "Oh, that. It was exceedingly ill-considered of me to go out of my way to attract Lord Heathbury. I did not think his devotion would be so great."

"Nonsense, you have enjoyed every moment of it," Lord Cheriton told her as he came up behind her. "Male adoration has never gone amiss with you."

He was accompanied by Lord Ratcliffe and inevitably Hattie and Kitty were close behind.

"I have been studying Lavinia's technique,"

Kitty admitted, "although I am still uncertain as to her *strategy*."

Lavinia's face grew pink as they all laughed merrily. "Indeed it was worth the hundred guineas it cost me," Lord Cheriton admitted.

"Poor Lord Heathbury is totally besotted," Hattie giggled.

"And so he should be," Sir Christopher retorted. "When Lavinia Merridew sets out to entrance a man he is *doomed* to adoration for the rest of his days."

"Oh, do stop funning all of you. I vowed you would eat your words, Cheriton, and if it is not a bitter taste I am sorry to hear it. I have succeeded in proving your cousin is not so different to any other man after all, which is all I intended to do. Indeed, he is merely unused to female company, that is all."

The men laughed merrily. "Oh come now," Lord Fairfax scoffed, "you will soon declare 'twas for his own good you set out to ensnare his heart rather than to salve your wounded pride."

She was about to retort in a like manner when she caught sight of none other than the object of their conversation who was standing on the first floor balcony. Her laughter died in her throat and her eyes clouded with pain at the sight of his stricken expression which told her he had heard every word uttered.

The laughter and conversation amongst the others died away as they too became aware of his presence. For a long moment there was only an awkward silence and then Lord Cheriton had the presence of mind to step forward.

"Good morning to you, Heathbury. Come down and join us do. We are about to break our fast."

The Earl looked from one to the other in silence and then his eyes finally came to rest on Lavinia who, convinced he had overheard most of their conversation, could only avert her face. Somehow she felt bound to meet his gaze and when she did raise her eyes to his she was shaken to see the fury there, a depth of emotion of which she would not have imagined him capable.

"You will have to excuse me," he said, stepping back at last, "but I must prepare to leave immediately. There is much to do at Heathbury and I have delayed here long enough."

He turned on his heel and they all watched helplessly as he went back to his room.

"He heard all that we said!" Kitty exclaimed, hardly bothering to hide her amusement.

"Oh, Theo, how awful," Lavinia cried at last. "I would not for anything have hurt him."

Lord Cheriton looked momentarily troubled and then he gave her a reassuring smile. "Nor would I, my dear, but what is done cannot be undone."

"But I must go and give him some explanation!" she protested. "We cannot allow him to believe we have been plotting together at his expense."

"But, my dear, that is precisely what we have been doing," Lord Ratcliffe said languidly.

Lavinia felt more wretched than on any occasion before and would have run up the stairs after the Earl only Lord Cheriton pulled her back.

"What is the use of flying into a pucker, Lavinia? His is not the first heart you have bruised, nor is it likely to be the last. Once you are in London and officially make your debut, hearts will be broken by the score."

Kitty tossed back her head. "It would not trouble me in the least, I assure you. He is deserving of a ribbing. I simply cannot abide anyone who is so ponderous and boring. I think Lavinia has been remarkably patient in enduring his company so often. A wounded passion can only do him good."

The others murmured their agreement but Lavinia still looked uncertain and Lord Cheriton was forced to put a comforting arm around her shoulders.

"Miss Stapleton is quite correct, you know. This may be the making of him as a man; every one of us has been wounded in the heart at sometime. Is that not so?"

He looked to the others for support and they murmured their agreement.

"I do not quarrel with that," she answered. "I just wish he had not overheard our funning. He is not in the least like us and does not know our ways."

This observation caused a murmur of agreement. Sir Christopher drew out his snuff box and took a pinch before saying, "Perhaps you *have* done him a kindness, Miss Merridew. This episode may just be the thing to set his resolve to remain a country gentleman for the rest of his life."

The others laughingly agreed and as they all made their way to the breakfast room in a jolly mood Lavinia still felt uneasy. Just before she preceded Theo into breakfast she glanced up at the first floor balcony where she had last seen the Earl, and then, determined to put the matter from her mind, she cast Lord Cheriton a smile and went into the room.

Four

At a certain hour on any afternoon the narrow paths of Hyde Park were always crowded with a fashionable array of people, some of them on foot but mostly exhibiting their elegant coaches or expensive horses—or both.

Riding along in one of Walter Lovell's barouches drawn by four fine horses was his wife Elizabeth and her sister Lavinia, the latter gowned in green velvet with a matching pelisse. Her hands were snug inside a sable muff and a beribboned bonnet framed her face prettily. Such excursions really were a triumph, for Lavinia was so much in demand. The carriage was obliged to stop every few yards so they could exchange words with all who importuned them.

Elizabeth looked almost as radiant as her sister, smiling and waving at an elderly lady in a carriage which passed them. "Lady Amshurst, Lavinia," she informed her sister. "Oh, her hat is horrid. Her sartorial taste is quite dreadful and always has been, but we must keep on good terms with her, for she is so influential."

She glanced at Lavinia approvingly as she acknowledged two bucks who paused before riding on reluctantly.

"Ah, I am quite taken back to my own debut, Lavinia. Of course, you would not recall it. You were still in the schoolroom."

"I do recall all the fuss and botheration."

"Enjoy it whilst you may, my dear, for once you are wed all will become mundane."

Lavinia laughed. "Not with the man I intend to marry. Life will remain exciting until the day I die!"

Her sister looked at her askance. "Lavinia, have you actually chosen your husband-to-be?"

"No! I doubt if I have even met him yet, but I can still dream."

Elizabeth smiled. "Not met him! I trust that you have. There are few enough young bucks not in love with you, certainly sufficient for a good choice."

"What I meant to say is that I am not in love with any of them—as yet."

"Lord Cheriton is very attentive, dear. I always thought you were too close to become lovers, but he seems quite determined that one day you should."

Lavinia frowned momentarily before her face cleared. "I do believe you are right. He is the dearest man and I dare say he would be a most indulgent husband. There is also the advantage in my knowing him so well; no pitfalls there, Eliza."

"No indeed. Oh, there is Amy Durrant. She is quite determined to marry Hattie off before you, but I doubt if it can be achieved. You have already laid claim to the hearts of every eligible man in Town."

"That is something of an exaggeration."

"Only a slight one," Mrs Lovell admitted, adjusting her pelisse and smiling sweetly at the woman under discussion whilst Lavinia waved to Hattie.

"The girl is as plain as a pipe stem," Eliza added when the carriage had passed, "although I doubt if that will signify. Lord Durrant is as rich as Croesus and Hattie's portion will attract some young buck I dare say." She glanced at her sister again. "If I had possessed your looks, Lavinia, I would have married a Duke—at the very least."

At this Lavinia was forced to laugh. "Oh, Eliza, you must have windmills in your head to say so. You and Walter have a rare happiness."

Elizabeth sighed. "I am the first to admit he is a mite prosaic, but he is so *very* indulgent. I think we are about to be approached by Lord Cheriton and Sir Christopher Bonham. They are such nice young men. Good day to you, Lord Cheriton, Sir Christopher."

The young men, both astride white mares, swept off their hats and bowed low in the saddle, chorusing their greetings. Both, however, had eyes only for Lavinia who dimpled prettily.

"What a pleasure it is to see two such lovely ladies on a day like this," Lord Cheriton greeted them.

"We have despaired of doing so this past hour," Sir Christopher added.

"When Miss Merridew is in London the heart of the Town beats the faster."

"You're a fool," Lavinia laughed and Elizabeth asked, "Do you always make such speeches when you meet ladies of your acquaintance?"

"Only the pretty ones, Mrs Lovell," Lord Cheriton assured her and then, addressing Lavinia once more, "I trust you will reserve a Scottish reel for me tonight at Almack's."

"Only if you promise not to trample my toes."

"When do I ever?" he retorted with mock horror.

"Always," Sir Christopher told him. "I am a much better dancer, am I not, Miss Merridew?"

"No, Sir Christopher, you are not," and then when they looked outraged, "But nevertheless I shall reserve a set for each of you. I do not forget my old friends."

"We shall make sure you do not," Lord Cheriton informed her mischievously.

Mrs Lovell acknowledged the wave of an acquaintance and it was then that Sir Christopher's jaw suddenly dropped in a manner unbecoming a gentleman of his standing. "Good grief!" he cried and the others followed

the direction of his gaze. "It cannot be.
Cheriton, I *am* wrong in what I am thinking,
am I not?"

Lord Cheriton's eyes opened wider, as if
he too could not believe what he saw. "No,
by jove, you are not!"

Mrs Lovell's hand tightened on the coachwork of the carriage whilst Lavinia's eyes
merely opened wide at the sight of the high
perch phaeton of the latest design, its yellow
paintwork gleaming in the sunlight. It was
cleaving a way through the crowds which
stopped to stare curiously at the phaeton
and its occupants, one of which was an
elegantly dressed lady of great beauty. At
her side, seated behind a team of coal black
mares, was a man attired in a sartorial
elegance which could be equalled only by
Beau Brummel himself. As the phaeton drew
level with Mrs Lovell's carriage the gentleman reined in slightly, long enough to raise
his curly-brimmed beaver to them all before
he set it back on top of his Brutus curls.

They watched it go and then to break the
astonished silence Mrs Lovell said, "Lord
Cheriton, that *was* your cousin Heathbury,
was it not?"

The young man still looked totally bemused

as he transferred his attention to her. "It certainly looked like him, Mrs Lovell, but it cannot be. Merely someone with an un-common resemblance, I fancy."

"Nonsense, of course it was he." Lavinia was still staring after the phaeton which continued on its elegant way through the park, exciting interest as it went. "I always knew there was more to that young man than you led us to believe."

"I assure you, ma'am, I know nothing of the matter."

Mrs Lovell was practically standing up in an effort to peer after the phaeton. "Who was the exquisite creature with him? Her hat was so elegant I am quite put out."

Lavinia was still in a state of shock at see-ing so fashionable and rakish a man in the place of the dullard she had known at Ardsley House, but now she transferred her bemused attention to Lord Cheriton who chuckled.

"Her name is Mrs Byefield. You may not know her . . ."

Elizabeth's lips drew into a narrow line. "Oh, so that is she. The young man is not so green as he would have had us believe."

"*Who* is Mrs Byefield?" Lavinia asked, breaking her silence at last.

Her sister did not answer and Lord Cheriton only cleared his throat in embarrassment. Lavinia drew in a deep breath. "A Cyprian," she murmured.

Sir Christopher smiled. "One has to admire his style. The Heavenly Byefield does not bestow her favours lightly. I have been laying siege to her door for weeks to no avail."

"I really do not think that fact is of interest to us, Sir Christopher," Mrs Lovell told him in an icy tone.

"My apologies, ma'am. Surprise has rendered me indiscreet."

Mrs Lovell clutched at her reticule and ordered the driver to move on. "Until tonight, gentlemen," she said, a mite sharply and the carriage jerked forward again.

The two young men raised their hats and for once Lavinia did not feel much like smiling or acknowledging them in any way. She stared unseeingly ahead of her, still greatly shocked at the change which had come over the Earl. It was inconceivable that it should have happened and yet it had, and it was something which a tailor alone could not achieve."

Elizabeth looked at her sister. "I was given to believe his interests were purely academic."

"So were we all, Eliza," she answered in a muted tone.

Suddenly Elizabeth's eyes narrowed and she said thoughtfully, "I recall the day of the picnic, Lavinia, when you returned with your gown all soiled and a tear in the hem. I found your explanation unsatisfactory then, but now I am quite concerned."

"What are you suggesting?"

"That Heathbury is not as green as I supposed."

Lavinia was forced to laugh. "Oh dear Eliza, we played hide and seek, and as always I chose to hide in a tree. Poor Heathbury was mortified at the notion. He was afraid of being alone with me at all and did his utmost to squirm out of the possibility."

Her sister nodded with satisfaction. "You relieve me greatly, but I cannot conceive why we did not know he had come to Town. I was given to believe he had no intention of joining us for the Season."

"That is what he led us all to believe." Her mind was full of the sight of him with that beautiful creature in the phaeton. Emily Byefield was well-known in the shady world of courtesans and she lived in great luxury provided by the wealthy and aristocratic gentlemen who beat a path to her door. She did not believe Sir Christopher was alone in his attempts to woo the woman. Her favours were hard-won by the most elegant and wealthy Corinthians, but Lord Heathbury . . .

Lavinia's sister was looking at her speculatively. "Despite your denial, there was a time at Ardsley when that young man seemed quite besotted by you. Now we are in Town, though and you have been presented . . . I wonder . . ."

Lavinia looked at her in alarm, her hands unconsciously clasping and unclasping within the muff. "No, Eliza! There is no likelihood at all!"

In the exclusive and hallowed confines of Almack's that evening the talk amongst Lord Cheriton's set was generally of the newcomer who had appeared in the Park that afternoon, for Lord Heathbury could not have chosen a better place in which to show himself. Few members of the *ton* would miss the afternoon ride or stroll in the Park.

As always Lavinia's programme was filled so she had little opportunity to quiz Lord Cheriton on the matter, although her thoughts had been full of it ever since the encounter.

Rachelle Edwards

At Ardsley House he had appeared such a dowd, a bore. No doubt he was still a bore, but his appearance certainly overshadowed that of any other man she knew. He was so handsome too. No other man succeeded in dressing with such perfection save Brummel himself.

Invariably it was Lord Cheriton who took her into supper and it was not until then that she could question him at last, but others were intent upon the same quest.

"Was it really your cousin we saw this afternoon?" she asked, shunning the supper provided.

His eyes were alight with mischief. "Indeed it was. Like you, dear one, I was doubtful, so after leaving the Park I cantered along to Mount Street and sure enough the house had been opened up. He has actually engaged Mr John Nash to rebuild it entirely and in the meantime lodges nearby."

Lord Ratcliffe, who had joined them, looked disbelieving. "I think we have all been the victims of a monstrous hoax."

"That is precisely my opinion," Sir Christopher added. "Heathbury and Cheriton have been laughing at us all for accepting the Banbury Tale they must have concocted together. You like your jest, Cheriton, and no doubt Heathbury does also."

Lavinia looked at Sir Christopher as did the others and the young man went on, "It occurs to me that Heathbury and Cheriton, whom we all know to be a quiz, decided to hoax us into thinking him a clodpole."

Lord Cheriton laughed. "Oh no, you are entirely wrong. I vow it and I was not gammoning you. Heathbury came off the boat just as you saw him at Ardsley. He brought with him trunks filled with just books. Once I recovered from the shock I offered to introduce him to my tailor, but he was not interested."

"Perhaps that was because he preferred to wait to patronise Weston, who undoubtedly makes for him now," Sir Christopher said dryly.

"Well, I am not entirely convinced," Lord Ratcliffe answered, taking a pinch of snuff. "He was seen at Gentleman Jackson's saloon in Bond Street yesterday and acquitting himself very well in the art of fisticuffs."

"The team pulling his phaeton today are magnificent. No daisy cutters they and he is said to have outbid everyone for those mares at Tattersall's," another young man informed them.

"It is rumoured that Brummel himself instructed him in the art of tying his cravat."

"What can he be up to?" Lord Cheriton asked himself aloud.

"Need he be up to anything?" Kitty Stapleton asked as she joined the group, smiling coyly at Sir Christopher. "He is just like all of us now and in my opinion 'twas merely a matter of time before it happened."

No one deemed to answer this but Lavinia's mind was still in a whirl.

"It is certain every toady in Town is ready to grease his boots." Hattie Durrant looked slyly at Lavinia. "Do you not wish you had taken him more seriously now?"

Lavinia turned away from her abruptly. "I do not know what you mean. Just because a man changes his coat does not mean he has changed his entire manner. I have no more interest in him now than I had at Ardsley."

Her voice was shrill because of exasperation, but at that moment a hush had fallen on the gathered company. Standing in the doorway was none other than the object of all the discussion, dressed once again immaculately, this time in a dark blue evening coat, wrinkle free and moulded closely to his broad shoulders. The muslin neckcloth at his throat was of pristine whiteness, contrasting starkly against his deep tan.

For a moment everyone stopped to stare and he appeared to be enjoying the experience, giving no indication that he had overheard what Lavinia had said although she was certain he must have done.

He had entered an exclusive circle into which one has to be born, and therefore newcomers were rare, so that whenever a stranger did appear on the scene he was treated with great curiosity and speculation. Lord Heathbury was certainly no exception and after taking advantage of the interest he had created he stepped forward to greet one of the lady patronesses, Lady Jersey, with whom he seemed on familiar terms.

His presence almost caused Lavinia to panic, for she had been assured that she was never likely to see him again. Now, any encounter must be fraught with the greatest embarrassment. However, Lavinia was saved experiencing any further discomfiture, for Lord Heathbury merely wandered around the room for some few minutes, only nodding briefly to the group of which she was a member, before passing on.

In all he remained at Almack's for only a short time, leaving when the dancing recommenced. Having recovered from her shock and surprise, Lavinia was beginning to suspect that his visit had been a deliberate ploy, simply to arouse everyone's curiosity, just as his ride in the Park had done in the afternoon.

Sir Christopher laughed when Lord Heathbury left Almack's. "No doubt the Heavenly Byefield calls!" he said ironically.

"Tell you what," Lord Cheriton challenged, "I'll wager he'll tire of all the tomfoolery within a sen'night and return for good to Norfolk."

"Done." Lord Ratcliffe answered laconically before going off with Hattie Durrant on his arm.

Lord Cheriton offered his to Lavinia. "Vastly diverting, is it not? Nothing quite so exciting has hit the Town since Lucinda Verity ran off with her father's house steward."

"That was not nearly so diverting as this," she replied, a mite sourly. "And you did assure me he and I were never likely to meet again. It could be embarrassing."

"Ah, but then I was not to know he would come to Town, but I am persuaded he has quite forgotten the incident, and so should you. As I said to Ratty, he'll tire of the fun in a sen'night."

Lavinia allowed him to lead her back towards the ballroom and although she was far from convinced she was also determined not to let the matter tease her any longer.

Five

Once again Lord Cheriton found himself the loser in a wager, for his cousin displayed no sign of tiring of the social round he once professed to abhor. Lavinia was still not called upon to speak with him, but nevertheless he managed to attend every event frequented by the *beau monde* and she saw him more often than she would have wished.

At Drury Lane he and an actress by the name of Daphne Oldencourt were seen to occupy the adjoining box to the one belonging to Walter Lovell, that evening occupied by his wife and her incredulous party. Everyone was talking about the newcomer and everything he did was noticed and remarked upon in detail, even to the extent of diverting attention from Mrs Siddons' excellent interpretation of the role of Ophelia.

Emily Byefield was seen with him once more at Vauxhall Pleasure Gardens this time and although Lavinia had decided not to be put out by him, his constant presence wherever she happened to be made that a difficult resolution to carry out. Happily the one type of event he appeared to be avoiding was the one where he would be called upon to stand up for the dancing and therefore no one of Lavinia's acquaintance was aware of her disturbed feelings. She took great comfort in the constant attention showered on her by the many young men who vied for her attention. A smile from her lips was greatly prized and a kind word sufficient to set them up for days. She encouraged admiration of this kind and flirted in the presence of male admirers which caused even more of them to be drawn to her like moths to a flame.

"Have you decided upon any of your suitors as yet?" Walter Lovell asked her one morning over breakfast.

Lavinia laughed. "Oh, it is far too soon. I am enjoying myself hugely, Walter."

"Marriage will not end that state of affairs," he told her. "At least, not if you choose wisely, and you do have more suitors than any young lady I have ever known."

"Then it is like I shall have a good many to choose from when the time comes."

"Lavinia prefers to keep them dangling," Elizabeth pointed out, "and quite rightly too. Cheriton is still persistent," she added, "and dare I say, the most genuine?"

"Theo is a dear, and I dare say I shall accept his offer—supposing he does make one after all."

"He will," Elizabeth answered, her mouth filled with bread and butter. "He is very sure of you and that is why he displays no haste."

"And when he does," added Walter, "you would be a sensible girl to accept."

Lavinia looked uncertain and then sipped at her coffee. "It is a comfort to know Cheriton is sincere and will always be there."

Walter sighed and then dabbed at his lips

with his napkin. "The match would have my wholehearted approval, needless to say." He glanced at his wife. "That visit to Bath was most beneficial, my dear. I do not feel quite so liverish."

"I am delighted to hear you say so, dearest." He got to his feet and as he walked to the door she added, "Do not forget we are to dine with Lord and Lady Kendle tonight. There is to be a ball afterwards."

He looked at first alarmed and then he grunted. "Walter does not relish the social life I fear," his wife complained after he had left. "He would as lief spend the evening at his club with his cronies."

Lavinia watched her sister eating for a few minutes and then cautiously asked, "Eliza, do all gentlemen keep a mistress?"

Mrs Lovell looked up slowly, her eyes wide. "Walter does not, if that is what you mean."

Lavinia smiled. "But Walter is not quite typical, is he, Eliza?"

The woman looked aghast. "He is quite normal I assure you!"

"Oh, Walter is the dearest man, but he is no rake."

"I should think not! I had no notion of marrying one, and if you possess the common sense I believe you have, you will follow my example. Truly, Walter is most abstemious and I do not have to tell you how rare a quality that is."

She hesitated a moment before adding, "If you are concerned about Lord Cheriton, Lavinia, let me say he possesses high spirits which are quite normal, and if it amuses him to patronise certain demi-reps it is of no account. He truly idolises you." She got to her feet. "And if you wish to add those blue ribbons to your bonnet we shall have to adjourn to the mercer's with no further delay."

Lavinia gazed thoughtfully at her cup and then, smiling at her sister, she went quickly to join her.

Hattie Durrant pushed her way excitedly through the crowds, glancing this way and that until she espied the person she was seeking.

Breathlessly she approached Lavinia who was being addressed by a young man eager to earn her favour. Lavinia had a gift rare amongst ladies of such tender years in that she was able to attend whatever was being said to her with great interest, therefore imparting to the other person the notion he was the only one in her world. It was not, as with so many, a deliberate ploy to ensnare male hearts, but a genuine part of her outgoing nature. In fact, at that moment she was not really listening; the ballroom was crowded and because she had been obliged to stand up for every dance since her arrival she felt exceedingly hot.

When she caught sight of Lavinia, Hattie Durrant gave the young gentleman a smile of apology and drew her to one side. "Have you seen who is here?" she asked in a breathless whisper.

For once Lavinia found her friend's coyness irritating and answered a mite sharply, "Really, Hattie, I have seen so many people this evening, as you can well imagine."

"Lord Heathbury is here!"

At that moment Lavinia had been adjusting her gauze shawl but she paused then before saying, "There is nothing remarkable in that. He attends most functions I note, but he will not remain. Heathbury, although he enjoys most other pursuits, eschews standing up for any of the sets. I do not believe he can dance very well."

"You are quite mistaken, Lavinia. This time he intends to stay!" The girl's eyes gleamed. "He has already stood up for the gavotte with Ariadne Chetwynd and she is quite moonstruck now; I am only surprised you did not see them." Lavinia's eyes narrowed in disbelief but Hattie went on regardless, "Not only that but he has been engaging others for the remaining sets, so it is obvious he intends to stay. I am to stand up for the country dance after supper. Imagine, Lavinia, we have quite mistaken him, you know. He is so very charming; I could scarce credit he was the same man who was at Ardsley. No doubt he will be engaging you at any moment."

Her eyes scanned the crowds anxiously, but there was no sign of the Earl. Lavinia snapped shut her fan, the loop of which she slipped over her wrist.

"If he does so it will be to no avail. I am already engaged for all the sets which remain."

"Oh, that is too bad, for it is becoming all the crack to be seen in his company."

Lavinia caught sight of the Earl just then. He was within a circle of young people and apparently holding them enthralled with some witty story.

"I cannot stand up with every man who

asks," she said testily, turning back to Hattie. "And I really cannot conceive why you believe I am at all interested in what he does."

The girl looked taken aback. "You were most certainly interested whilst we stayed at Ardsley."

Lavinia twirled her fan airily. "He was a challenge, Hattie, nothing more. Once I had won his heart he was of no further interest to me. As I have observed on a previous occasion, a change of clothing does not signify a change of nature."

"You are more fickle than I supposed, Lavinia, heartless too. What you did was quite cruel."

Lavinia's eyes opened wide. "You minx, Hattie Durrant! What I did was to behave kindly towards him, which no one else was prepared to be, and it was certainly to the amusement of such as you."

She turned away, her breast heaving with indignation and it was opportune that Lord Ratcliffe came to claim her hand for the next set. But it was all she could do to sparkle as usual, especially as she was aware of the Earl nearby on the dance floor, partnering Kitty Stapleton who looked rather smug and pleased with herself.

One thing which was very apparent—he had turned the theory of dancing into very good practice, for she could not fault his performance at any of the sets, all of which he stood up to with a different young lady.

As the evening progressed Lavinia fully expected him to approach her and it was irksome when he did not, despite the fact that she did not wish to stand up with him at all. It would only be embarrassing to them both and yet it was still annoying to know that his avoidance of her was bound to be commented upon. She could feel it. It would be inconceivable to most present at the ball that the Season's most eligible bachelor should not at least pay lip-service to the most popular heiress.

On several occasions as she partnered others Lavinia found herself actually facing him in the set. He said nothing to her and she avoided looking at him, but whenever her eyes met his they seemed to be mocking her. His hands were cool on hers and she let them go as soon as was possible, but his steps were sure, and she could not help but admire his style.

"Your cousin seems to have discovered the ability to enjoy himself," she told Lord Cheriton when they went into supper later that evening.

"I confess I sadly misjudged him, Lavinia. Ratty has won the small wager we had and I shall not embark upon any more on his account, be assured. I just cannot get the fellow's measure. Father is delighted, of course. He had him marked as a rustic but it seems the fellow learns fast."

Lord Cheriton glanced across the room to where, as was usual now, his cousin held court to any number of admirers. "He is planning to hold a ball of his own, you know."

"No, I didn't know," she answered in a muted tone, fearing that she would not be invited, which would be very damaging to her social standing.

"His house in Mount Street is at present filled with masonry and workmen and cannot be put to rights before the end of the Season, so Father has offered the use of ours. Heathbury feels the need to reciprocate for the way he has been welcomed into Society."

Lavinia gave a harsh laugh. "He cannot be so simple. Welcomed! Of course he was. There is not a single family in our circle which does not have at least one unmarried daughter. Has he no notion how eligible a bachelor he is?"

"Oh, make no mistake, my cousin is fully aware of his importance, especially now that Prinny is pleased to receive him at Carlton House." He glanced again at the Earl who was unaware of the discussion and he added, "It suits him well, I own, but I fear he could easily become too top-lofty."

Lavinia made a great deal of adjusting her gauze shawl. "He cannot give a ball without a hostess."

"Mama has offered to perform that office on his behalf. She could do no less, naturally." He smiled at her then. "You look a trifle pale, my love. I do hope the amount of activity in which you are indulging of late is not proving too much for you."

She smiled at his concern. "It is merely somewhat hot in here. Do you not think so?"

"Lady Kendle does not believe in opening windows, I'm afraid, but if you feel unable to continue I shall inform Mrs Lovell of the fact, and you must be taken home."

She was quick to pat his hand reassuringly. "There is no need for that, dearest. I am perfectly hearty, but I will take the opportunity of putting a little more rouge on my cheeks."

He got to his feet at the same time as she. When she cast him a quick smile it was disconcerting to discover he was gazing at her in a way to which she was unused. "You need no paint, Lavinia."

"You are very kind to say so," she answered demurely, still disconcerted.

"In fact, you are incredibly lovely," he went on quickly, as if such speeches embarrassed him.

Inexplicably her eyes filled with tears. "Oh, Theo, you are such a dear."

He continued to gaze at her. "Would that you may always regard me so."

"You know that I will."

Her mind was still filled with emotion when she hurried out into the hall where a number of people were enjoying the comparative cool. Amongst them was Lord Heathbury who was laughingly in conversation with Ariadne Chetwynd. The girl simpered and fluttered her fan in response to whatever he was saying to her. Lavinia hesitated for a moment as the Earl looked at her and then she hurried up the stairs to the dressing room set aside for ladies to attend their needs. Lord Cheriton's words echoed in her ears, confirming that he was indeed in earnest about her, but despite a mutual devotion Lavinia was strangely reluctant to encourage a closer attachment.

Several ladies were there when she arrived and they all greeted her. For once she felt not the slightest bit sociable, yet, as she seated herself before a dressing table, she was able to declare lightly, "La! What a crush."

"I declare this is the best ball of the Season," remarked one young lady as she preened herself.

Lavinia eyed her coolly. "That would discount your own come-out ball, Dolly."

The girl turned on her heel and flounced out of the room to the chuckles of those who had overheard. "What a goosecap that girl is," remarked another. " 'Tis no wonder she is obliged to sit out most of the sets. The difference tonight is that Heathbury stood up with her for a country dance. I don't doubt this ball is better even than her own!"

Lavinia began to apply a little rouge to her cheeks with a hare's foot just as

Kitty Stapleton seated herself next to her.

"Your gown is simply heavenly, Lavinia. I am quite carried away with envy."

"How very kind of you to say so. You seem to be enjoying yourself tonight, Kitty."

The girl drew a deep sigh of contentment. "I feel quite wonderful. Do you not think Lord Heathbury the most perfect partner?"

Lavinia closed her reticule with a snap. "I have yet to stand up with him, so I cannot judge."

The other girl's eyebrows rose a fraction. "You are surely engaged to stand up with him later."

"No. He is too late if he wishes to approach me."

Kitty Stapleton's eyes were wide. "How strange that is. It is a most uncommon occurrence, for everyone else importunes you first."

"It would have made no odds," Lavinia answered airily. "I have been engaged for every set since long before he arrived. I cannot admire any gentleman who arrives late at a function and those who do so cannot expect to be partnered by me."

"Ah well, dear Lavinia, that at least is

good news for the rest of us," the girl replied brightly.

Lavinia managed to smile despite her chagrin. "Dear Kitty, you must excuse me; I hear the music and I am engaged for this set."

Kitty smiled too. "When are you not, Lavinia?"

She laughed as the girl preened her curls. "Rarely, Kitty. Rarely."

She rushed out of the room, her smile fading. The minx, she thought. She knows only too well that Heathbury had not as much as acknowledged her presence that evening and was revelling in her discomfiture. And Kitty Stapleton was only one of many who would derive the greatest possible satisfaction out of the situation. Lavinia's mind seethed with fury, so much so she could not return to the ballroom without revealing her chagrin.

Even though she was well aware someone was waiting to partner her she went through one of the card rooms and out onto the balcony instead. The cold night air felt good on her cheeks which were burning with indignation. It made no odds that he ignored her at this function, but if such behaviour repeated itself at the many others to come she would be a laughing stock. She hardly dared to contemplate that they might not receive an invitation to the Earl's own ball. Her entire social life would be ruined, and that would devastate Elizabeth.

The night sky rocked above her at the realisation that he meant to do this to her. It was to be his revenge on her; a humiliation to match his own.

Lavinia owned that she deserved it, but it was nevertheless going to be hard to bear.

A familiar giggle caused her panic to subside momentarily as she saw a flutter of white emerge from the shrubbery. Peering into the darkness Lavinia recognised Ariadne Chetwynd, her only rival in looks although most were agreed that it was Lavinia who was the prettier of the two.

It was frowned upon to make secret assignations and as this appeared to be one Lavinia was more than a little curious as to discover with whom the girl dallied in the shrubbery and she stood very still after shrinking back into the shadows. Ariadne giggled again and whispered to the man who emerged from the garden walk with her.

The light streaming from the windows of

the house shone onto his golden curls, brightening the stark whiteness of his shirt. Lavinia stiffened as Lord Heathbury took the girl's arm and guided her back into the ballroom. When they had gone she let out a long sigh. So that was the way of it. He and Ariadne made a handsome pair, she was forced to admit, and the girl would always nourish his self-esteem.

A footstep on the balcony caused her to turn on her heel and she managed to smile wanly at Lord Donoghue, her partner for the set she had sought to avoid.

"Miss Merridew, I have been seeking you everywhere. The sets are being made up."

Lavinia immediately went towards him. "Do accept my apologies, Lord Donoghue, only it was so stuffy indoors. Once I came inside I quite lost all notion of time."

"That is perfectly understandable, but," he added with a smile, "having waited patiently the entire evening for the honour of standing up with you, I was not about to give it up."

His words, together with his adoring look, was balm to her hurt pride and she threw back her head and laughed merrily.

"Nor shall you be obliged to, Lord Donoghue."

Foolish, she chided herself, to allow one man's malice to blight the happiest year of her life when there were so many adoring of her. From now on, she vowed, she would overlook the Earl's presence as completely as he ignored hers.

Six

"All these balloon ascents become rather trying after a while," Elizabeth complained as her open carriage entered the gates of Hyde Park. "The first few, I recall, were exciting but I cannot conceive why we are here today."

"Because everyone else will be here, and this one is different," Lavinia informed her. "Monsieur Gaillard is to jump out."

"He will break his neck and I am not at all certain I wish to witness it."

Lavinia laughed. "He is using a device to ensure he does not injure himself. A piece of material, Cheriton tells me, which traps air beneath it and slows the descent to safe proportions."

"Dear me," Elizabeth murmured. "Whatever shall we see next I wonder? I do trust that Boney will not hear of it or we shall be descended upon by a thousand Frenchies all jumping from balloons."

She laughed at her own joke and then pointed to where the crowds had begun to gather around the, as yet, earthbound contraption.

"I see that Lady Gleneagle's party has arrived. Dunnet," she ordered the driver, "to the left if you please." Then she turned to her sister once more. "I see Lord Cheriton's curricle too."

Lavinia turned in her seat, her face breaking into a smile of recognition. "So it is. That coachwork is unmistakable. He just will not believe me when I say it is too garish. I can see from here that he is talking with Lady Gleneagle. She does tend to din his ears."

"I am well aware of Lady Gleneagle's failings, dear. More to the point Cheriton was speaking to Walter for some time at his club last night—mainly about you, may I add."

Lavinia looked at her sister curiously as Elizabeth went on. "It seems Cheriton is allowing you time to enjoy the Season before making an offer, although he has made it quite clear he is in earnest over you. Walter has told him he has our approval, naturally, but is he not the most thoughtful creature? How many young men would exhibit such patience in the face of love?"

"He is most uncommon," Lavinia agreed, "and I cannot be sorry for it. I am being vastly diverted by all that we do and I must confess," she added with a gurgling laugh, "I do enjoy having so many men in love with me."

"So I have observed," her sister answered dryly. "I feel quite sorry for them when I see the way you devastate them with your charm and then give them no hope for the future. And you do it so well, dear. No doubt they will recover as did poor Lord Heathbury, although why I should refer to him so I do not know. He is far from being the pathetic mooncalf I had decreed him to be."

Lavinia's ready smile faded somewhat, for

thoughts of that gentleman invariably caused her discomfort. "I sincerely hope you did not voice that thought in public," she said, suddenly anxious.

Elizabeth looked rather uncomfortable. "Well, I was having a coze with dear Polly FitzWilliam whilst we were at Ardsley one evening when I happened to say so to her, adding that you would in all probability treat his heart heedlessly as you did with all the other young bucks."

"I trust he was out of earshot at the time."

"Naturally I believed that to be so, but imagine my prodigious amazement when he arose from a nearby chair seconds later and fixed me with such an expression I really cannot describe. I grew quite cold."

Lavinia groaned. "Oh, Eliza, when did this occur?"

The woman adjusted her bonnet fussily. "I cannot quite recall; a day or two before we left Ardsley for Bath I believe."

Lavinia was still feeling disquieted as her sister peered across the field and waved to her friends. "Lord Cheriton, good day to you! Perfect weather for an ascent, do you not think?"

As soon as the carriage came to a halt Mrs

Lovell gave her sister a meaningful look before climbing down and going to join her friend. Immediately she had done so Lord Cheriton came across to the carriage where Lavinia dutifully remained.

She was gowned in blue velvet with a matching sable-lined pelisse, and knew the ensemble became her well. The young man gazed at her for a moment or two and she looked back at him from beneath the brim of the feather-trimmed bonnet which framed her face prettily.

"I have been impatiently awaiting your arrival," he told her.

"You honour me indeed," she answered with a smile. "And it is good to see you, Theo."

One eyebrow went up a fraction. "I could boast of those words in all the clubs. A kind word from you is much prized, Lavinia." His words caused her cheeks to grow pink and she was glad when he looked around him before saying, "It is a long-drawn out business waiting for the balloon to be made ready."

"Everyone believes on this occasion the wait is justified."

"Most certainly. This huge crowd is assembled just to see this poor fellow break his neck."

Lavinia laughed. "I know. Is it not famous?"

"It is what the fellow hoped for." He looked at her for a long moment again. "Incredible as it seems, you appear to grow more lovely with every passing day."

Despite being accustomed to rich compliments she felt that her cheeks were flooding with colour once more. "I am beginning to believe you are just another toad-eater."

"Where you are concerned you must never believe that, my dear." He paused once again before adding, "Your brother-in-law and I had an uncommonly amiable coze last night . . ."

She fixed her eyes on the balloon which was being inflated slowly, and hoped that she feigned indifference well enough. "Oh, yes . . ."

Lord Cheriton placed his hand over hers which curled around the side of the open carriage. "I told him of my feelings for you, my wish to marry you . . . He seemed not at all surprised, I am gratified to say."

She looked at him boldly then, employing her usual flirtatious attitude. "Theo, have you offered for me?"

"I know how much this Season means to you, Lavinia, so I would not offer for you at this stage. However, I have made it very clear that I shall marry you when you are ready. Your brother-in-law, I am delighted to say, approves wholeheartedly."

Her eyes grew round. "I am not altogether certain *I* approve of your sureness, Cheriton. I may never be ready to marry you. There are so many with a claim to my heart."

"Not as valid as mine," he said with maddening complacency. "Lavinia, my dear love, flirt as much as you wish, but you are most certainly mine."

She challenged him with her eyes. "You are so very certain of yourself, my lord."

He smiled. "We have known each other since we were mere babes on leading strings, and I have always been sensible of the fact that you and I were meant for each other. My decision was made many years ago, when you were a skinny child with long legs like a pair of pipe stems."

"How ungallant of you!" she protested, stifling her laughter. "You will have to do far better than that to win *this* heart."

He raised her hand to his lips. "Oh, my darling love. I adore you. The very ground you walk upon is hallowed to me. I will kill any man who presumes upon my love."

Lavinia laughed delightedly. "That is doing it too brown! I'm persuaded your attic's to let and you are only fit for Bedlam."

He straightened up as a brightly painted phaeton pulled up in front of the Lovell's carriage. Lavinia's laughter died in her throat and Lord Cheriton said, "I thought Heathbury wouldn't miss this." He waved his hand as his cousin climbed down from the phaeton and handed the ribbons to his tiger.

Lavinia bit her lip but when Lord Cheriton offered her his hand she climbed down from the carriage. The Earl was strolling slowly towards them, nodding briefly to those of his acquaintances who called to him.

"Good day to you, Heathbury," Lord Cheriton cried. "Great fun, this. Prime bit of blood you have there," he added, nodding towards his cousin's horses.

"I fancied you would think so," the Earl answered smilingly.

Standing between the two men who towered over her, Lavinia felt uncharacteristically self-conscious, steeling herself for the snub she feared about to come.

"Acquainted with Miss Merridew, are you

not?" Lord Cheriton asked of his cousin.

Lavinia raised her eyes at last and found that he was looking at her quite expressionlessly. "Oh yes," he said softly. "Indeed I am."

She was forced to avert her face once more, unable to gaze for long into those deep blue eyes. It was then that a number of other people of their acquaintance wandered up to them and before very long Lavinia, for once, found herself not the centre of attention. In addition, Heathbury's presence somehow robbed her of the will to demand the attention to which she was accustomed. Mute, she listened to the usual bantering which took place between them with Lord Heathbury holding court. It was a most unusual state of affairs.

At last she could bear it no longer and, unnoticed, wandered away. Her sister was seated in Lady Gleneagle's carriage with Lord Cheriton's mother, the Duchess of Ardsley, and Lavinia had no real desire to join them either so she wandered off to where the balloon was being made ready for its ascent.

After a few minutes she glanced back the way she had come to see the Earl standing a full head above all the other men. Her friends were clinging on to every word he uttered. Every now and again a roar of laughter would erupt, carrying easily to her. Even Theo did not seem to have missed her. Just at that moment she hated them all.

Other amusements were taking place whilst the balloon was being made ready; there was an organ-grinder and monkey, whose antics were creating some amusement, and jugglers of amazing dexterity. Lavinia watched them all in turn, putting a few coins in their boxes in appreciation. Pedlars of every kind mingled with the crowd, the more successful being those who offered refreshments, drinks of lemonade and hot pies which smelled delicious. A bear dancing at the end of a stick was causing great amusement amongst the crowd and there was even a man, who for the consideration of a few pence, would milk the goat he led around on a string.

There were other pedlars too; those who would sell gew-gaws to those growing bored with the waiting. Lavinia waved away several of them until a young gypsy girl offered her a tray of ribbons and would not go away.

"Buy my pretty ribbons, lady. Only six pence. That's nothing to a grand lady like you."

"No, thank you," Lavinia answered firmly.

"Let me read yer palm then. I can tell your fortune, that I can. You'd like to know what Fate has in store, wouldn't you, m'lady?"

"I am not interested. Go away."

She began to move away, but the girl caught at her arm, which alarmed Lavinia, for the girl no longer looked amiable. Before she could protest further a resolute voice said, "Unhand the lady, you miserable wretch, or I'll give you the whipping of your life."

The girl immediately let go of Lavinia's arm and hurried off into the crowd whilst wide-eyed Lavinia whirled around to find the Earl towering over her. For moment she stared at him in astonishment and then, when the shock subsided, she retied the ribbons of her bonnet, in order to give herself a little time to recover her surprise.

Avoiding looking at him directly, she murmured, "I am obliged to you, Lord Heathbury."

She was uncomfortably aware that he looked amused at finding her in an awkward predicament. "Really, Miss Merridew, you ought to know better than to mix with the rabble; it is most unwise."

105

"I . . . needed a little exercise after riding in my sister's carriage."

"It appears to me you are not enjoying this outing."

She looked up at him sharply then. "I cannot imagine what makes you think so, Lord Heathbury." Her head went back proudly. "I find everything vastly diverting."

His lips were curved into a mocking smile. "How refreshing to hear you say so. I had the distinct impression you were bored."

"Not with the proceedings, Lord Heathbury," she answered with a great deal of relish, averting her face so he could not see her smile.

There was a momentary pause before he said, a trifle stiffly she noted, "Will you allow me to accompany you back to your sister's carriage?"

"I much prefer this vantage point. However, I am certain your acquaintances eagerly await your return so pray do not let me detain you any longer."

"You do not do that, Miss Merridew. This is my first balloon ascent and I admit to feeling as awed as a child."

She looked at him curiously as he gazed eagerly to where Monsieur Gaillard had climbed into the basket. "I confess I did not look to see you in London after our conversations at Ardsley House."

"I hope," he said, giving her his attention again, "that you were not too put out by my change of heart."

Her shoulders lifted into a slight shrug. "Why on earth should you think so? What you do or do not do is of no consequence to me, I assure you."

"Yes," he answered through his teeth, "I gathered that at Ardsley."

An old crone bearing bunches of flowers came hobbling up to them. "Flowers for the lady, m'lord, pretty flowers for a pretty lady."

He glanced at Lavinia momentarily and his lips quirked into a smile. Then he tossed a coin at the crone and took from her a bunch of violets.

"A handsome pair the two of you make, m'lord," she said before hobbling away.

"How very flattering of her to include me in her praise," he murmured as he presented the violets to Lavinia.

As he did so his eyes met hers and her heart began to pound loudly, so much so it seemed it might rise into her throat and choke her.

Quickly she drew her gaze away from his to look at the violets, almost unseeingly. "They are my favourite flowers."

She was glad at that moment to see the ropes being untied, this claiming his attention once more. That gesture had been so unexpected it had shaken her to the core of her being and she was glad he had been distracted so that he could not guess the confusion it had created in her. A gasp arose from the crowd as the balloon floated unsteadily upwards on the light breeze.

"Ah, a perfect ascent," he told her. "The first I have ever witnessed, would you believe?"

When it was certain the balloon would not fall to earth again Lavinia gave him her attention again, looking at him mockingly.

"Such diversions as you have indulged in of late, Lord Heathbury, leave little time for Greek philosophers, I fancy."

Nonplussed, he returned her smile with equanimity. "That is indeed true, but such are the attractions of Town life I confess I haven't missed them at all."

When he stepped back apace Lavinia's mind was filled with visions of Emily Byefield, sitting at his side in the phaeton in the Park or on his arm at Vauxhall Gardens.

"I trust you feel free to return to your sister now, Miss Merridew. If this madman intends to jump out of the basket, it would be as well for you to be safely away from the immediate area."

She laughed before saying demurely, "Your concern is most flattering, Lord Heathbury."

He led the way back to where the carriages were standing. A diminutive figure at his side, Lavinia managed to keep up with his long-legged stride. For a minute or two they walked along in silence and then she said breathlessly, clutching the bunch of violets in her hands:

"Lord Heathbury, I beg that you will allow me to explain about what happened at Ardsley . . ."

He halted abruptly and Lavinia bit her lip when she dared to look into his face. His eyes had narrowed slightly.

"I am not sure I understand. Explain? What can there be to explain? I believe we all enjoyed ourselves thoroughly."

Lavinia might have guessed he would not make apologising an easy task for her and she lapsed into silence, not knowing how to continue. Indeed, she was exceedingly sorry she had even tried.

Moments later they resumed walking and he said in a bright conversational tone, "I recently discovered an interesting fact, Miss Merridew; your late father was Sir Harry Merridew, was he not?"

"Why, yes," she answered in some surprise.

"It seems that he was a great friend in his youth of my own father."

"That is a coincidence," she replied, her mind still awhirl.

"Had my own father remained in this country, we might also have grown up in each other's company."

"It's an interesting supposition and I dare say it would have been so."

Cries and gasps rose from the crowd and both Lavinia and her companion turned on their heels to look upwards. She cried out to see the Frenchman plummeting through the air and unconsciously gripped onto the Earl's coat sleeve in terror. Then as if by magic a piece of cloth fluttered in the air, ballooning out to slow the man's descent.

Lavinia drew a sigh of relief and smiled at

the Earl. "All ends happily," he told her, his lips curved into an ironical smile.

She realised then that her fingers were still clutching at his sleeve and in great embarrassment she let it go, stepping back abruptly.

"I was quite terrified out of my life," she admitted, laughing foolishly.

He clucked his tongue. "Such concern for a mere performer, Miss Merridew. You have quite a soft heart after all."

She gave him a sharp look, wondering if he were being sarcastic, but just at that moment she caught sight of Lord Cheriton hurrying towards them. Never had she been more pleased to see him and she started forward gladly.

"Cheriton, was it not so exciting?"

"Lavinia, my dear, I beg you not to be alarmed, but Mrs Lovell is unwell ..."

Her ready smile faded and she hurried even more. "Eliza? What is wrong? I beg you to tell me."

Lord Cheriton's arms flapped uselessly at his side. "I do not know. Just a swoon, I think. She was overcome by the excitement."

"Never," Lavinia answered in a breathless

voice, hurrying back towards Lady Glen-eagle's carriage. "Eliza has never swooned in her life. There must be some other explanation."

All three of them made haste and when they arrived at the carriage there was a crowd around it. They made way for Lavinia who arrived in time to see her sister being ministered to by the Duchess of Ardsley who was holding a vinaigrette to her nose.

"Eliza!" Lavinia cried, unaware that the violets had dropped from her hands to the ground. "Oh, my dear, what has happened?"

"Nothing alarming," the Duchess told her. "Merely a swoon. She will soon be recovered."

"Stand back everyone," she heard Lord Heathbury order. "Allow the lady some air."

Amazingly his command was immediately obeyed.

Mrs Lovell was looking rather dazed at this point and Lavinia said, "We must get her home immediately. Eliza, can you manage the few yards to your carriage?"

The lady looked too bemused to answer and it was again the Earl who said, "Stand aside, Miss Merridew. Permit me to attend to Mrs Lovell."

Before anyone had a chance to realize what

was happening or protest against it he had lifted Elizabeth into his arms and was carrying her back to her own carriage. Still very frightened and bemused Lavinia followed close behind, climbing into the carriage and cradling Elizabeth in her arms once she had been set down in the seat.

No one seemed very much surprised when Lord Heathbury pushed Mrs Lovell's driver to one side and took up the ribbons himself. Lavinia was forced to admit he was a better driver and had them back in Manchester Square the quicker. At that moment she could only be glad of it.

Seven

Lavinia could not keep still. She subsided onto a sofa only to jump up again and pace the floor, heedless of the servants who were attempting to light the candles in sconces and chandeliers.

"Now, there really is no cause for you to get into this pucker," Lady Gleneagle told her reprovingly, having followed in her own carriage and insisted on waiting, together with the Duchess of Ardsley, to hear what the physician had to say.

"The physician is a very long time," she complained. "Do you not think it has been an unconscionable time since he arrived?"

"They charge such enormous fees, my dear, they like to be seen to earn them," the Duchess informed her. "I'll wager there is nothing wrong with your sister save an attack of the vapours."

"Eliza was never vapourish," Lavinia complained, wringing her hands together and glancing, not for the first time, at the carriage clock on the mantel.

"We can all be in certain circumstances," murmured Lady Gleneagle, who then turned to the other woman. "I must own, Griselda, your nephew has turned out to be quite level-headed. At first I judged him to be as dizzy as most other young bucks of his generation."

"I would not have agreed with you a month or two ago, but I must own he surprises me agreeably."

Lavinia's nerves were stretched taut and this further flattering discussion almost made her scream. His name was on everyone's lips. Mothers hoped he would pay court to their daughters, girls only waited to be addressed by him, and men of substance and fashion openly admired his style and solicited his friendship. Lavinia just wished he would return to the obscurity from whence he came.

"I recall meeting his Mama once," Lady Gleneagle went on. "Shy, timid creature, not at all old Heathbury's style although it appeared he did adore her."

The drawing room door flew open and Walter Lovell came hurrying in. His face was strained and Lavinia was full of fear.

"Walter, what is the news?"

He gave her a fleeting smile, nodding to the other ladies at the same time. "She is quite recovered and naturally angry at such a botheration on her account."

He wiped his perspiring brow with his handkerchief and Lavinia said, "That is a great relief, Walter."

"Did the physician diagnose what caused her to swoon?" Lady Gleneagle enquired.

"Excitement," the Duchess insisted.

Walter Lovell went to a side table where he poured a measure of brandy from a cut-glass decanter, something rarely seen, as the war had virtually put an end to fresh supplies.

"Walter?" Lavinia said in alarm. "It is nothing serious, is it? You would not seek to gammon me on this?"

"It is a serious matter, and yet it is not."

"Walter!" She was growing more alarmed with each second that passed.

He patted her hand. "Lavinia, dear, I really don't know how to say this but Eliza, your sister, she is . . . well, she is . . ."

"Ha!" cried the Duchess. "Mrs Lovell is increasing! I knew it all the time! Did I not say so to you, Fiona?"

Lady Gleneagle shot her a disgusted look. "No, Griselda, you did not."

Walter Lovell still looked totally bemused. "After seven years of marriage, I cannot, as yet, credit it."

"Some produce after nine months of marriage and yet others take much longer," Lady Gleneagle pointed out, nodding sagely.

The news took some few moments to penetrate Lavinia's fear-filled brain and then she let out a cry of joy, hugging her startled brother-in-law tightly.

"Walter, that is the most wonderful news! Eliza, dear Eliza. How clever she is! This means our children will be able to grow up together! It is what I had always hoped."

Lady Gleneagle frowned at her, saying, "I had no notion you were even betrothed, Lavinia," at which her excitement became a little more muted, although she felt inclined to giggle.

"There is a problem," Walter went on after gulping back the brandy, "which troubles Eliza greatly."

"Problem?" Lavinia was afraid once more.

"To be brief it concerns you, my dear . . ."

"Oh, *I* could not be more delighted, Walter."

He continued to look uncomfortable. "The physician has warned us in no uncertain manner that Eliza must rest. No late nights or grand entertaining . . . Lavinia, this is your come-out year . . ."

At last she understood what he was trying to say, but before she could comment the Duchess got to her feet. "Pray tell Mrs Lovell she need have no more qualms on that score. She is to rest and not endanger her health in any way. *I* shall undertake to chaperon Lavinia. Mrs Lovell can be quite certain her sister will gain entry to all the most important functions."

Before either of them could reply the Duchess had swept out of the room with Lady Gleneagle in her wake. The moment she had gone Walter, who still looked rather bemused, turned to her.

"That is a remarkable piece of good fortune, Lavinia. You could have no greater patroness than the Duchess."

"I know," she answered thoughtfully.

He went and poured another glass of brandy. "This news is altogether too new for me to be able to think properly. Eliza wishes to see you, Lavinia. She charged me to tell you that, so do go to her before she gets into a pucker."

Lavinia needed no more urging and hurried to the door, but then she began to laugh. "Have I said something which amuses you?" Walter asked, looking mystified.

"I have just realised that she must be furious not to have seen Monsieur Gaillard land."

"Oh, indeed she is," Walter assured her. "The first thing she asked of me when she was able was for news of the landing. How he contrived not to break his bones I cannot conceive . . ."

As Lavinia hurried up the stairs her amusement and pleasure faded somewhat. She couldn't be anything other than overjoyed at her sister's splendid news and she had always regarded Theo's mother fondly, but the prospect of being chaperoned by her was not altogether an attractive one at that moment for it was bound to bring her into closer contact with the Earl of Heathbury. That prospect caused her to feel both alarm—and excitement.

It transpired that she saw him no more frequently than before, but on every occasion once again he reverted to his earlier attitude and behaved as if she did not exist, save the times when it was absolutely necessary for him to acknowledge her. Not once did he engage to stand up with her at any of the balls and routs at which they found themselves attending, although he rarely missed one set himself.

Ariadne Chetwynd was his most frequent partner and tongues were inevitably beginning to wag. Lavinia found his indifference insufferable as his aunt's official patronage of her should have weighed with him, if nothing else did. For so eligible a man, whose name was on everyone's lips, to be seen to be indifferent to her was most damaging to her standing, she felt.

The fact that he had bought violets for her in Hyde Park counted for nothing as no one of any consequence was witness to it, and pride forbore her to boast of it to Ariadne

Chetwynd who lost no opportunity of voicing her delight at the calls, posies and presents of sweetmeats he sent round to her house, not to mention—which she did at every turn—the attention he showered upon her at all times.

Lavinia was almost resigned to the way he was punishing her—after all she lacked no number of adoring *beaux* to salve her pride—when one afternoon whilst she was at the Duchess's Grosvenor Square house, Lord Heathbury himself came striding into the small drawing room.

She looked up at the door as it opened, expecting to see either Lord Cheriton or his mother and her heart began beating in the ridiculous manner she resented whenever he was present.

He too seemed taken aback to see her there and hesitated in the doorway. "Miss Merridew, I did not look to see you here."

"No doubt," she answered, smiling slightly and turning away.

"I was told my aunt was here, for it is she I was actually seeking."

Lavinia pressed her clasped hands to her breast as if that would still its heaving. "She was, Lord Heathbury, until a few moments ago when she went to speak to the house-keeper. She will be returning quite soon, I am certain."

Seemingly satisfied, he came right into the room at last and she affected to return her attention to her previous task.

"You appear intent upon an onerous task," he said, coming up to where she was seated at an inlaid secretaire.

She laughed lightly. "Oh, it is not that. I was merely sorting through the many invitations the Duchess has received of late, so that she can arrange her journal."

"From the look of that considerable pile of invitations it would seem that you and my aunt would scarce have a moment to spare."

"You must also find life similarly busy," she answered, moving the cards about unnecessarily.

"That is indeed true, otherwise I would have called in at Manchester Square to enquire after your sister's health. I trust she is fully recovered from her indisposition."

He moved round to the front of the desk which was scarcely less disturbing. "Oh, she is much better now," she told him, giving him a quick smile. "Did you hear of her condition?"

"I had heard, and it must be delightful news."

"She so much looked forward to this Season, but she is quite resigned now to her enforced rest. She lies on a day bed, eating marchpane and reading novels, and all her acquaintances call in at frequent intervals so she misses none of the on-dits."

"I am certain she can rest easy knowing you are in my aunt's good care."

None better, Lavinia thought wryly. The Duchess had married off Theo's three exceedingly plain sisters into three of the most influential families in the land through sheer determination.

Conscious of his disturbing scrutiny she applied herself to her task once more and it was with relief she greeted Lord Cheriton a few moments later. He looked surprised to find his cousin, who because of his close proximity to Lavinia, could be seen to stiffen very slightly. An odd expression came into his eyes; it was almost one of coldness, but Lavinia did not know him well enough to judge and fancied that she might have been mistaken.

Moments later he was smiling urbanely and greeting his cousin warmly.

"We do not see you at Grosvenor Square nearly often enough," Lord Cheriton told him. "What do you find to occupy yourself of late?"

"Need you ask in front of a young lady?" Lord Heathbury answered.

"Enough said," Lord Cheriton replied laughingly, "although I do not envy you, Heathbury." He came up to Lavinia then. "I am the luckiest man alive. I would not wish your sister ill, but I cannot be sorry to see you so much more often."

Lavinia laughed in embarrassment. "We do not see each other any more often than we did before."

Next to join them was the Duchess herself who came into the room clutching the week's menus. "Ah, Heathbury, dear boy, I was told you had arrived."

The Earl quickly crossed the spacious drawing room, although it was the small one for daily use, and kissed his aunt on her cheek. "Aunt Griselda, how handsome you look."

"You are almost as great a flatterer as your dear late father, but not quite," she said in a reproving but nonetheless pleased tone of voice. "I take it you are anxious to fix a date for this ball you're intent upon giving."

"I feel it is the least I can do after all the hospitality I have been shown."

The Duchess gave a ghost of a smile. "You think it remarkable, do you?" She laughed then. "I was mighty hospitable to bachelors myself when I had the gals at home. Now," she went on musingly, "Lavinia has been kind enough to go through the events of the next few weeks and I regret nothing can be fitted in until the fifteenth of next month."

"Then the fifteenth it shall be," he answered lightly. Then starting towards the door, "Make arrangements as you see fit, Aunt, and send all the vouchers to me. I know I leave it all in good hands."

Lord Cheriton started after him. "Trotting off to a mill at Hampstead shortly. Care to join us, Heathbury?"

The Earl hesitated before saying rakishly, "Sorry, Cheriton, can't be done. I have other fish to fry." He smiled at his aunt. "Good day to you, Aunt." His gaze lingered some- what frostily on Lavinia then. "Miss Mer- ridew."

As he went out of the door Lord Cheriton said mischievously, "I recall there used to be a time when his greatest desire was to visit Athens. Now the farthest he wishes to travel

is to Mrs Byefield's establishment in Blooms-
bury! Time I was off too," he added cheerfully,
waving to them both as he hurried out.

"I worry about that young man," the
Duchess confided after they had both left.

Lavinia looked up at her anxiously, "Theo?"

"No!" his mother answered with a laugh,
"My nephew, Heathbury."

Lavinia looked bewildered. "I cannot conceive why, Your Grace."

"Oh, it is foolish I dare say, but his behaviour worries me."

"It is no more outrageous than others."

"Oh, of course it is not. My son, for instance, is a true Corinthian, but Heathbury
is quite different. All he does nowadays seems
totally out of character."

"Have you paused to consider that how he
was before might have been more out of character? How he is now is more like to be his
real self."

The Duchess looked visibly more cheerful.
"I do believe you are quite correct, my dear.
He worried me so before, I should be only too
pleased he has turned out to be a bang-up
blade after all. His youth was so very odd,
you know. My brother died young and poor
Arabella was so painfully shy. She just could

not face the social round here in England and was far more at home in her native plantations."

"I cannot understand that, Your Grace."

"Nor can I, I confess. Here there is so much which is diverting. There—nothing. Arabella could not help her nature, but it was a pity for the boy. She would never allow him to come to us."

The Duchess gazed at Lavinia thoughtfully for a moment before adding, "Whilst you were all guests at Ardsley, I suspected he had formed an attachment to you, Lavinia."

Her cheeks coloured and she looked away, hating to be reminded once again of an incident which had become shameful in her mind.

"I think not, Your Grace."

"Well, I did consider your outgoing ways were just what he might need, but that state of affairs would have displeased my son, not to mention several others." As Lavinia looked at her again the Duchess smiled. "Oh yes, I am well aware of Theo's passion for you. It is the one thing which has remained constant in him."

"I am . . . very fond of him too," Lavinia admitted.

"You make a very handsome couple. I only

hope Heathbury does as well, and I suspect that he will. He and Ariadne Chetwynd may yet make a match of it." Sighing suddenly she handed Lavinia a wordy sheet of paper. "This is the guest list for my nephew's ball. You would do me a great kindness if you would pen the invitations."

"It will be my pleasure," she replied, relieved to see an end to a conversation which threatened to become a mite uncomfortable.

As she picked up the quill she could not help but chuckle to herself. At least there was no longer any fear that she would not be invited to the function being referred to already as the Ball of the Year. Of course, it was equally certain that he would ignore her presence there, but Lavinia was growing accustomed to that.

Eight

On the night of Lord Heathbury's ball at the home of his aunt and uncle, the roads converging on Grosvenor Square were choked with carriages, with link boys lighting the darkness all around. Every window in the mansion blazed with lights and music drifted from the ballroom, down the curved staircase and into the street.

Guests would still be arriving for some time to come, but Lavinia had been present since the ball had commenced, although she too would have preferred to arrive late given the opportunity. Being so close to the Ardsleys did have its drawbacks as well as its advantages.

"Ariadne Chetwynd is in high feather nowadays," Hattie Durrant observed to Lavinia as the girl, together with her parents arrived. "And," she added in a whisper, "we do not have to look very far to comprehend why."

She gave Lord Heathbury a a sly glance, making her inference quite clear. He was standing at his aunt's side, still greeting the guests who came up the stairs in a never-ending stream.

"She should not," Lavinia mused, "be certain of anything, for I do not believe Heathbury is always in earnest."

"Neither is she! As a flirt she is second only to you, Lavinia, but perhaps we are all in for a surprise on this occasion. He always engages her to stand up for several sets which does indicate he has fixed his interest. Nobody engages *me* for more than one!" She gave Lavinia a curious look then. "I cannot conceive why he should prefer Ariadne to you, though. He really did seem moonstruck at Ardsley. I'm persuaded it's because he overheard our funning at his expense."

Lavinia was forced to draw a sigh. "*That* was a very long time ago, Hattie, and I must remind you that Ariadne and I are not in competition for *anyone's* affection."

Hattie Durrant looked outraged. "I did not suggest that you were, my dear. Everyone is fully aware you are far too interested in a possible dukedom to consider a mere *earl*," she added before flouncing into the crowd.

Once again Lavinia drew a sigh, for she was certain Hattie would now inform all those who would listen that Lavinia Merridew was becoming too top-lofty by far.

As was usual, however, she was not left on her own for long. The moment Hattie had left she was accosted by several young men, all anxious to engage her for the coming sets. She was laughing and conversing with some of them not too far from the doorway when Lord Heathbury came into the ball-room at last to join his guests. The Duchess was on his arm and momentarily Lavinia's eyes met his before he deliberately turned away to smile at Ariadne Chetwynd who had contrived to be nearby at the precise moment. Lavinia turned her back on them both and gave all her attention to those anxious to flatter and divert her.

Gowned in palest green satin, decorated with seed pearls and her dark hair curled around a diamond tiara, Lavinia was sensible of her own charm and needed no one to tell her she was radiant. She had taken pains to ensure it would be so, and it did add to her confidence.

"The Duchess seems to have outshone herself on her nephew's behalf tonight," remarked Kitty Stapleton, glancing around her at the splendid setting of the ball.

It was an opinion that so many others had voiced since arriving that evening. The ballroom had been transformed into the facsimile of a summer garden, with real greenery swathed around marble pillars and swept across the roof to resemble arbours. The several arches formed by all the greenery led up to, at the far end of the ballroom, a fountain which spouted not water but champagne, a supreme extravagance in these days of war against the French. Whereas most houses were conserving jealously their stocks of French wines, Lord Heathbury was using his with a careless abandon which caused his guests to gasp in admiration.

The group of young people chattering excitedly around Lavinia slowly made their way towards the fountain, only to be joined by an ebullient Ariadne Chetwynd. It was generally held that it was only a matter of days—hours perhaps—before Lord Heathbury approached Sir Harry Chetwynd with an offer of marriage. Looking at her now, immaculately gowned and quite breathtakingly lovely, Lavinia still could not see her as a suitable match for the Earl, although she was ready to concede she along with everyone else constantly misjudged him and had from the very beginning of their acquaintance. He had turned out to be so inscrutable in every way there was no method of knowing his true likes and dislikes, or feelings.

"La! What a crush," she declared, swishing a mother of pearl fan to and fro. "Did you ever see such magnificence? Anyone who is not invited here tonight may consider themselves *finished*."

Lavinia looked at her with amusement, despite her misgivings which she realised were purely on Lord Heathbury's behalf. "It is evident you are thoroughly enjoying yourself, Ariadne."

"It would be difficult not to, my dear

Lavinia. Everything here is of the finest, and as always Heathbury's attentions are leaving me breathless. I scold him constantly and remind him that he is being unfair on all others who wish to pay me court, but he will not heed my strictures in the least. Only last week I found a basket waiting for me at home and inside—what do you think?"

"I cannot imagine," Lavinia answered feigning boredom.

"A white kitten! What do you think to that?"

"Perhaps a hidden message, Ariadne dear," Lord Cheriton answered, much to everyone's amusement.

The girl's face twisted into a vexed expression before she flounced away. Lavinia became serious again. "That was a trifle hard on her," she told Lord Cheriton.

"Nonsense, the girl has windmills in her head if she believes Heathbury is in earnest."

"Everyone else believes that to be so too."

"It suits him to make much of one of the prettiest of this Season's chits, but I cannot see someone as serious-minded as he spending the remainder of his life leg-shackled to a goosecap like Ariadne Chetwynd."

Lord Ratcliffe was leaning against a pillar

and as he took a pinch of snuff he remarked laconically, "He has no need to; once the honeymonth is over there is always Mrs Byefield and other such divine creatures to divert him."

"Besides," Sir Christopher broke in, "Heathbury was only interested in classical studies before he began to notice that young ladies are a different species to ourselves. He ought to be more thankful to Miss Merridew for that revelation, although from all I observe he seems exceedingly reluctant to acknowledge the debt."

Feeling extremely discomforted as always when the subject was broached Lavinia said, "I believe you have all exaggerated that incident out of all proportion."

"He followed you around like a mooncalf," Kitty told her mockingly.

"I'll wager you wish he would do so now," Hattie Durrant put in, a little spitefully, having rejoined the group.

"There you are wrong," Lord Cheriton answered before she could think of a cutting answer. "I should like to remind you all that I am the only man in Lavinia's life."

The eyes of the other two girls opened wide. "Well," said Hattie, "I do declare that is a most revealing statement, Lord Cheriton."

"That brings us considerable relief, for *we* can now make our choice from those who are left," Kitty added in a coy tone.

Moments later they hurried away, giggling between themselves and Lavinia drew Lord Cheriton to one side.

"Theo, what a foolish thing to say. By the end of the evening the entire gathering will be expecting an announcement."

He gazed at her fondly. "It can be made as soon as you give the word, my love. I am growing weary of watching other men pay court to you and not being able to say a word to stop them. There are wagers being placed in all the clubs as to who will win your hand and although I am a clear favourite, my patience is growing thin."

At some other time she would have been amused at the notion, but at that moment she looked away, not knowing what to say. It would be difficult to explain that she was just not ready to become betrothed. The Season was in full swing, she enjoyed the attentions of so many, and there was Elizabeth to consider. The celebration of a betrothal and the activities leading up to a wedding were quite beyond her at that time, but because she had anticipated them for so long Lavinia was most reluctant to commit herself before her sister was able to cope. But at the back of her mind was a fear that perhaps they *were* only excuses.

"Theo . . ." she began and he smiled and patted her hand.

"All right, my dear, I do understand. We shall discuss the matter at another time."

Lavinia had little chance to draw a sigh of relief before he said thoughtfully a moment later, "There are times when I feel quite strongly that my cousin has never forgiven us for our behaviour at Ardsley."

This observation caused Lavinia to be newly alarmed, this time for a different reason. "I am sure I don't know what you mean. Has he spoken of it to you?"

He smiled. "Naturally not. For a man of his manner and address it would be demeaning, but I am certain it is so. Since he came to London I have felt, naturally, that we have more in common now. He has developed into quite a sporting fellow, but every attempt I have made to get closer to him has been rebuffed. Oh, in not so many words, but he always has something else to do when I suggest he joins our diversions.

I have ceased to approach him of late."

Although the room was stiflingly hot Lavinia suddenly felt cold and drew her shawl about her.

"I attempted to apologize to him once, but he professed not to know what I was talking about and I truly believe that must be the case. We are feeling guilty for no good reason. After all we have not served him ill in any way."

The young man smiled again. "You speak very wisely, my dear; it is Mama who voices the opinion that I should have a closer relationship now. I cannot call him a bore or a clodpole, and we pursue the same interests, but in truth, Lavinia, he is more of a highflyer than I."

She laughed and it was at that moment a young man came to claim her hand for a promised set. From then onwards she stood up for several more with various partners although the pace was hectic she did notice that Lord Heathbury had not for once taken the floor with Ariadne Chetwynd, for the girl had several different partners too. Nor was there any sign of his unmistakable figure anywhere in the ballroom and Lavinia assumed him to be in one of the cardrooms.

From all she had heard of late he had become addicted to the game of whist and was now a skilful player.

At the end of several sets she was not only hot but exceedingly thirsty too. She returned to the area of the champagne fountain, seeking out Lord Cheriton to whom she had promised the next set, but he was nowhere in sight and she watched with some amusement the antics of those who were already feeling the effects of the ever-flowing wine.

Suddenly a familiar figure loomed in front of her. Wearing a well-fitting dark blue evening coat and a brilliantly white lawn shirt, Lavinia needed no one to tell her Lord Heathbury was the handsomest man in the room; the most elegant too and her heart began to thump despite her attempts to still it.

"Allow me to procure a glass of champagne for you, Miss Merridew," he offered, so gallantly she was immediately suspicious.

There seemed to be a gleam of amusement in his eyes which served to discomfort her further. She was more used to gentlemen regarding her adoringly.

"I do not usually drink wine, Lord Heathbury," she murmured.

"But you must—tonight."

"Do you intend for me to become foxed?" she asked challengingly.

"There is no need for you to go to extremes, Miss Merridew. One glass will not go amiss."

So saying he dipped a glass into the fountain and then, wiping it carefully on the napkins provided, he handed it to her before filling one for himself.

His paying her the slightest attention was so totally unexpected that she was at first lost for words but then she raised her glass in salute.

"Congratulations, Lord Heathbury. You have succeeded in outshining every other host and hostess this Season."

As she sipped the unfamiliar drink he said, looking at her from beneath his lashes, which she noted were surprisingly long and dark, "Is that not the idea, wherever a function is held? Not to provide a diversion for one's friends and acquaintances, but to outdo everyone else."

Although further discomforted she smiled, "You are gammoning me now."

" 'Pon my honour I do not," he declared with mock indignation. "Well, perhaps only a little, and I'll wager you are unused to anything other than flattery."

For the want of something better to do she continued to sip her drink. "You have a poor opinion of me, Lord Heathbury, which I am certain I deserve so I make no protest."

She put down her empty glass as a liveried footman passed with a tray and would have moved away from him only the Earl said, "If that is what you desire I shall flatter you, Miss Merridew, and it will not be empty words." She continued to walk away when he added softly, so only she could hear, "You look magnificent and it is no exaggeration to say you eclipse every other woman here tonight."

At this Lavinia paused and then turned to look at him in alarm, seeking signs of mockery in his manner but there was none and her heart began that ridiculous thumping again.

"Your praise is extravagant," she protested, averting her eyes.

"There is not one man in this room who would not agree with me."

It was with mixed feelings that she saw Lord Cheriton approaching them. When he caught sight of her his face broke into a smile of pleasure which warmed her. No confusion there, she thought. His eyebrows rose a fraction when he noticed she was in conversation with his cousin.

"Wonderful evening, Heathbury," he said, slapping his cousin on the back. "This ball will be talked about for a long time to come."

The Earl eyed him appraisingly. "I'm gratified to hear it, Cheriton, for that is the notion I had in mind. Your Mama, I own, has done handsomely."

"Oh, come now, Heathbury; Mama has hosted many a function but none so grand as this."

"Again I am gratified to hear it." He paused to survey his cousin once again before saying, "I believe you are due to call on me tomorrow, but in view of the late hour at which we are likely to retire tonight may I suggest we postpone the visit for a day?"

Lord Cheriton's face, to Lavinia's surprise, grew rather pink as he glanced at her before replying in a strangled tone, "Er . . . yes, as you wish, Heathbury." Lavinia was still puzzled when he looked at her again, saying a mite hurriedly, "Lavinia, I believe the sets are being made up for our country dance."

But before Lord Cheriton could claim his partner the Earl had stepped between them. "Cheriton, it is my considered opinion that you are far too proprietorial over Miss Merridew and as host tonight I am sure you won't mind if I claim the sets you have already bespoken." His eyes sparkled with merriment as he added, "After all, it is still in the family."

Both Lord Cheriton and Lavinia were far too surprised to make any protest, and mutely she allowed the Earl to lead her onto the floor, but as she glanced back in some bewilderment at Lord Cheriton he was glaring after them, his face still suffused with colour.

"Lord Heathbury, that was very shabby of you."

He looked not the slightest bit abashed. "But, Miss Merridew, the end result in gaining you as a partner is worth a little shabbiness. Cheriton will recover his disappointment, I assure you."

Aware of the speculative eyes which were upon them, Lavinia could only be glad he was at her side. She held her head up high, knowing they made a handsome pair. His dancing, as she had previously observed, was very good and she wondered how many hours he had been obliged to practise to perfect the steps.

Not content with depriving Lord Cheriton of her partnership by subtle means of cajolery and charm he managed to persuade all her other partners to relinquish their call on her, and before long stares followed them everywhere and tongues could be seen to be wagging. Whenever she and Lord Heathbury passed Ariadne Chetwynd the girl looked to be in high dudgeon, which was not altogether surprising.

The Earl did not relinquish his proprietorial hold on her until supper was served. Lavinia, by that time, hated to admit to herself that she did not wish him to leave her side, but he was obliged to go and speak to as many of his guests as he could. As Lavinia watched him exercise his considerable charm over everyone he approached, she could only marvel how well he had overcome his shyness.

Lord Cheriton pushed his way through the crowds at the supper table to return with a plateful of food for her.

"Quite a hurricane," he murmured, handing her a plate and a napkin, "but one must admit the evening's an undoubted success."

He glanced at her. "I don't even resent the fellow being proprietorial over you."

"Really, Theo?" she said in a chiding tone, unable to eat the food he had brought her for excitement. "And I believed your feelings were true."

"You know that they are. Don't have to keep making flowery speeches, do I?"

"Yes," she answered in a muted tone.

"Thought you weren't such a flibbertigibbet. Send you a posy in the morning then."

"Thank you," she answered with heavy irony.

"Anyhow, it does prove you were quite right; he does not bear us any ill will. Don't want to be on the outs with my own cousin, you know." He looked at her again, swallowing a mouthful of food, "as long as he doesn't make a habit of monopolising you, that is."

Lavinia laughed but as soon as the music struck up again the Earl was at her side.

"Really, Lord Heathbury, you are causing quite a stir," she protested when he fended off yet another erstwhile partner. "If you insist on partnering me for every set, we shall only succeed in setting every tongue a-wagging."

"Ah, but consider how boring the tattle-baskets will find the morrow if we do not give them something to talk about."

"But you have other guests . . ."

He gazed into her eyes before leading her into the next set. "Have I? You surprise me, Miss Merridew. I believed there was only the one."

Her heart suddenly soared like a dove, and from that moment onwards her feet did not seem to touch the floor. As they scarcely paused for breath between sets it was indeed as if there were only the two of them in the room.

Nine

"Ah, dearest, I was so hoping you would come in early to see me today."

Lavinia walked into her sister's sitting room where Elizabeth was lying on a day bed, a shawl about her shoulders and a rug over her knees. Her condition was very apparent now.

"How are you today, Eliza?"

"Oh, very robust, my dear. In fact I feel quite a humbug lying here day after day."

Lavinia hurried across the room, stooping to kiss her on the cheek. "You must not think of doing otherwise."

Elizabeth sank back into the cushions. "I will not. This child is too precious for me to behave rashly, but I do regret seeing your Season go by with so little participation. There will not be another for me to enjoy, for you are far too handsome not to become leg-shackled before the start of the next one.

"You do look very handsome today, dear. Your gown is quite lovely. I recall our choosing the material together. Now, do sit down and tell me all about Heathbury's ball. I am in a fidge to hear every on-dit, and I did hope it would be you who was first to call in for a coze."

Lavinia sank down at the edge of the day bed and took Elizabeth's hand in hers, hardly able to contain her excitement. "Oh, Eliza, it was the most wonderful evening! I cannot recall ever enjoying another more."

Mrs Lovell looked quite taken aback at such fulsome praise. "Lavinia! It must have been a truly wondrous occasion for I have never heard you talk so."

"I cannot say less, dearest, for it was most

magnificent, as you will, no doubt, hear from everyone else who was present."

"Then do not delay! Tell me everything about it!"

Obediently Lavinia went on to describe the decorations in the Grosvenor Square House, the sumptuous supper in which every dish was a set piece following the theme of a summer garden, fruits made to look like flowers and sweet confections appearing to be flower beds. Lavinia's voice softened when she went on to tell her sister of the splendid firework display which she had seen from the terrace with Lord Heathbury at her side, and the release of a thousand caged doves into the night sky. Elizabeth was anxious for her sister to describe the fashions worn, and they spent a good many minutes laughing at the graphic picture Lavinia's account conjured up.

"It certainly seems to have been quite an extravagant affair, although I am persuaded Heathbury can well afford it."

"I am only sorry you missed it, dearest."

Elizabeth chuckled. "No more than I, Lavinia. Tell me, were you engaged for every set as usual?"

Lavinia smiled to herself at the memory which she was certain would live on in her mind for ever whatever the future held. That was something on which she dare not even speculate in her most private thoughts. Up until last evening the future had never included the Earl, but now . . .

Nothing in her manner revealed her inner torment and excitement when she answered, "Yes, indeed. I was not obliged to sit out one."

Her sister sighed with satisfaction. "It is no more than I would expect. It will not be long before Walter is besieged with offers for you. So many have already approached him tentatively, but I do hope your chosen husband will be patient enough to wait until after my confinement to marry you. That is the one event I have no mind to miss."

"As if I would consider marrying anyone without your presence," Lavinia chided. "It's unthinkable. Any man who wishes to marry me will have to contain his ardour that much longer."

"Love is impatient," Elizabeth sighed.

Lavinia's eyes gleamed as she recalled dreamily being out on the terrace so close to the Earl. Naturally, they were not alone but no one else mattered. Even hours after the ball had ended she still felt isolated from the rest of the world, caught in a strange bubble of happiness which suddenly surrounded her.

Her sister was looking at her curiously when the Duchess of Ardsley was announced. Lavinia took the opportunity of standing up and moving away from that probing gaze, for she was not yet ready to admit her feelings which were far too new and wonderful to share even with her own sister. She was well aware, however, that a succession of visitors would be only too anxious to acquaint Elizabeth with news of all that had happened last evening.

The Duchess swept into the room in the imperious manner she invariably employed. It usually impressed those who knew her and cowed those who did not.

"Eliza, my dear, you look quite splendid."

She bent to kiss Elizabeth's cheek as she said, "Thank you, Your Grace. How kind of you to call."

"Tush. You must not be allowed to lose touch with all that is happening in this town."

Then the Duchess cast an eye over Lavinia who bobbed a courtsey and immediately averted her face. "I did not expect to see you up so early, Lavinia." She turned to Elizabeth again. "Your sister scarce paused for breath last night. She sparkled even more than the champagne, which is to say a great deal."

Lavinia went to gaze out of the window which faced on to the square, where the Duchess's horses were being exercised by the grooms.

"So she has been telling me, Your Grace. The ball, I am given to understand, was a most uncommon success."

"My nephew fully intended it to be so. Whatever he intends to do nowadays he invariably does well."

Her words invoked the memory of Lavinia's conversation with the Earl in the library at Ardsley. He had said something very similar to her too, and she only wondered why no one had realised what a very determined young man he had always been.

"But all credit for the success must needs go to you, Your Grace," Elizabeth was saying.

"Not so, I regret. 'Twas all Heathbury's idea. I merely executed his instructions." She glanced at Lavinia at last. "I assume Lavinia has told you he monopolised her entirely last night. No other young man was allowed to intrude."

Elizabeth's eyes narrowed slightly as she glanced at her sister who in turn appeared abashed. "Our discussion had not reached that point when you arrived."

"Well, I can assure you it was so. Everyone is commenting upon it as you can imagine. I cannot move more than a few steps without someone accosting me to remark upon it to me." Once again she glanced at Lavinia who although her cheeks had grown slightly pink continued to gaze out of the window. "It is sufficient to turn any girl's head."

"Your Grace, I assure you nothing your nephew may say to my sister is like to turn her head. She possesses an uncommon amount of sense which is far beyond her years."

If only you knew, Lavinia thought to herself.

The Duchess smiled as Lavinia silently twisted her hands together, the only outward sign that anything was amiss. "I am glad to hear you say so. I am exceedingly fond of my brother's boy, but of late I have been at a loss to understand his behaviour. It is almost as if he were eccentric." She gave a harsh laugh. "Which, if it were true, should not be so surprising; his Mama was an exceedingly queer fish in my opinion. Ah, well," she sighed, getting to her feet, "I must move on. My mantua maker is waiting. Lavinia, I shall see you tonight for dinner before we remove to Vauxhall. If I were you, my dear, I should spend the most of today resting. You don't want to look done-up tonight."

Lavinia smiled faintly and would have followed the Duchess from the room only Elizabeth, inevitably, called her back.

"Dearest, is it really true you stood up with Lord Heathbury for *every* set?"

She drew a sigh. "No, Eliza! I did stand up with others, but," she added, averting her eyes, "it is true Lord Heathbury did engage me for most of the latter part of the evening. I was never more surprised in my life."

Elizabeth gazed at her curiously again for an uncomfortable few moments. "When you came in here this morning I sensed there was something different about you. Now I suspect that Heathbury is the cause."

"No!" Lavinia cried, laughing harshly. "That is not so, Eliza."

"You are not in love with him, are you?"

Lavinia put one hand to her head which throbbed slightly. "Of course not. Just because he engaged me for once for several sets does not automatically indicate I should be in love with him—nor he with me."

"You are one of the few in this Town who is not."

Exasperated now Lavinia retorted, "As you told the Duchess yourself, Eliza, I have far too much sense to act so foolishly. Let all the others throw their caps over the windmill, but I wouldn't be such a chuckle-head. The man's an out and out rake."

"And dedicated to it by all accounts. Heed your heart, my dear. You have but one to give, so choose the recipient wisely."

Lavinia gave her sister a curious look then. "You . . . once seemed to favour him as a suitor. Do you not recall that?"

"Oh, yes indeed, because he seemed so attached to you at Ardsley, and it was before he began his hellrake pursuits in earnest, I may add. There are those who would care only to be Countess of Heathbury, but for you there must be more than a title and a fortune. You could not live in that kind of marriage anymore than I, Lavinia."

"But are not all men rakes in their youth, Eliza?"

"Naturally, but not with such dedication as the Earl of Heathbury. Only think of his behaviour since he came to Town. Of late he persuaded poor Ariadne Chetwynd of his devotion. Do you really not recall that? I'll warrant the poor chit was quite discomposed yesterday evening."

Lavinia turned around and smiled reassuringly at her sister. "Your warnings are to no avail, dearest, so please do not bother your head on my account. You know very well I will be sensible and not lose my head because of a few charming words."

Mrs Lovell, however, did not look quite so convinced but she smiled in response as Lavinia kissed her on the brow.

"I believe I shall heed Her Grace's advice and rest for a while. I want to appear my best tonight when so many of my suitors will be present."

As she went out of the room the warnings were far from her mind already and she smiled to herself in anticipation, for the Earl had made a particular point of asking if she would be at Vauxhall. She did not doubt that he would be present too and despite the warnings she could not help the excitement which rose in her heart at the prospect of seeing him again.

Ten

A great many people had already converged
on Vauxhall Pleasure Gardens by the time
the Duke and Duchess of Ardsley's party
arrived at their reserved box in the Rotunda.
Several guests invited to join them arrived
shortly afterwards, all of them full of exciting
comments about the Earl's ball.

"No need to ask if you had a famous time,"
Hattie Durrant said slyly, and Lavinia's
cheeks grew pink.

She was glad that the artificial light in the form of hanging lanterns hid the fact that she was blushing.

"Miss Merridew was undoubtedly the success of the evening," Lord Ratcliffe added, eyeing her morosely. "Heathbury has the devil's own luck. I cannot engage you for more than one set in any evening."

"You are obviously asking the wrong person," Hattie told him. "I should always stand up with you whenever you asked."

"I know," he answered heavily, which caused them all to laugh, drowning out the music being played in the Rotunda.

"The answer to popularity, Hattie," Kitty Stapleton told her sagely, "which I have often observed, is not to be so readily available."

They all looked to Lavinia who had remained silent for an unusually long while. She had, in fact, been daydreaming and not listening to any of the idle chatter going on all around.

"One thing everyone is agreed upon and that is the way you put Ariadne Chetwynd to shame last night. It was as though she were sitting on thorns. I, for one, can not feel sorry for her; she is too top-lofty by far."

"I assure you I meant to do no such thing.

Indeed, Ariadne was not obliged to sit out any of the sets last night."

Lord Cheriton moved closer to her. "I beg you all not to tease her any more. My cousin is a notorious rake and not to be taken seriously."

"We are not taking him seriously, dear boy," Sir Christopher answered with a grin. "One just has to admire the fellow's style in selecting one chit and making her feel like . . . well Queen of the May. It might never happen again but it is an occurrence they will recall with pleasure for the rest of their days."

"Lavinia would not be such a goosecap to heed his flummery," Lord Cheriton retorted. "She was merely being polite to her host. Is that not so, my dear?"

She forced a smile to her face. "I do not care with whom I stand up as long as I have a partner, otherwise I should be obliged to dance on my own which would look a trifle odd."

The others laughed at her joke but then Kitty declared, "Would that Heathbury chooses me for his attentions next."

"Tush!" her friend retorted. "You almost swooned when he merely cast a word at you at Lady Dunnington's rout last week. Should he choose to flatter you, you would have an attack of the vapours!"

"Indeed, you talk about yourself!" Kitty told her indignantly.

"Oh, can we not speak of something else?" Lavinia appealed when she could bear it no longer.

On many a previous occasion she had enjoyed such conversations when it concerned someone else but she was fearful, should it continue, that she would not be able to feign indifference for much longer.

The Earl had yet to make an appearance, which did not altogether surprise anyone. Invariably he arrived late at any gathering to which he was invited, no doubt in order to create the best effect. It was a common enough practice and because it was so often employed Lavinia was surprised anyone arrived anywhere at a reasonable hour. Tonight, however, she was impatient to be in his company again and it was all she could do to hide that fact from her friends.

Her mind returned often to the question Eliza had posed that morning. Was she in love with him? Lavinia knew that if she was not she was certainly experiencing something

162

quite wonderful. But it was love that she felt
for him; there was really no doubt about it.
Having returned home from the ball only in
the early hours, she had spent the remainder
of the night wakeful, reliving the entire
evening in her mind from the moment he
had first spoken to her by the champagne
fountain. Anything that had happened before
was of no consequence at all. She pictured
every nuance in his manner towards her and
each word he had uttered. Every hour of the
day seemed like a lifetime to be endured
until she was able to see him again. It could
only be love, she reasoned, which caused her
to feel this way, and she was certain it had
not begun last night. The start of her infat-
uation with him had begun months ago—in
the library at Ardsley House.

Lord Cheriton caught her eye and she was
forced to look away quickly as guilt assailed
her. Since the events of the previous evening
she had hardly dared to think of him. Dear
Theo and his hopes for the future. Thoughts
of him now blighted the feeling of wonder
which she was certain must hover around
her like a halo.

"Let us take a stroll before supper and
admire the decorations," Lord Ratcliffe sug-

gested, and the others were quick to endorse.

Normally the suggestion would have found favour with Lavinia too, but on this particular night she wished only to wait for the Earl to arrive. Needless to say, though, she acquiesced and under the indulgent eyes of the older people in the party they wandered off together.

After walking round the Rotunda, to exhibit their fine apparel to acquaintances present and pausing to speak with a few of them, the party wandered off into the illuminated walks where more of their friends were to be found. Further away were darker corners where harlots and cutpurses lurked, but the young bucks were mindful of the females and avoided those places until such times when they were alone.

"Did you see such an ugly gown as the one Greta Handinge was wearing?" Hattie asked and Kitty replied, "Only if one disregards the puce satin Felicia Cooper wore last night. I do not believe anything could be more unbecoming than *that*."

They chuckled merrily together and Lavinia drew a sigh. So continued the continual backbiting which she could only find childish now. She moved closer to Lord Ratcliffe who looked down at her and said, "This gathering ain't so much to your liking, is it?"

Lavinia smiled wanly. "I never did like Pleasure Gardens, but when the Duchess of Ardsley is one's patroness it does not do to protest."

"Good Lord no!" he exclaimed with a laugh. "Forceful lady, Her Grace. And I must say there are places I would rather be tonight."

"Alas there is no racing at night, Ratty," she teased.

"It is far beyond time to arrange a meet. The course would have to be lantern lit, of course, but I do not believe it is beyond possibility to do so."

"I understand you have had considerable luck at Epsom recently, Ratty."

"Just as well, my dear. My pockets were well and truly to let a sen'night ago."

"You couldn't have been in dun territory, not you of all people."

"Worse than that, you know. I was foolish enough to beg the blunt off Heathbury to pay the duns, and then *he* started to dun me too. Oh, in the most charming way, of course, but dun me he did. It was a mite disconcerting. I owe a deal to a filly by the name of Jocasta."

Lavinia was thoughtful. "Ratty, does Heathbury make a habit of stumping the blunt for anyone who asks?"

"Don't know about anyone, Miss Merridew, but he said he would be glad to stump the blunt for any of Cheriton's cronies, and heaven knows we all need it from time to time. He's the only one ever to be in funds, although we're all at a loss to know how he manages that with his outgoings. Parsimonious father I understand. Close as wax by all accounts."

"Does *Cheriton* beg the blunt from his cousin, Ratty?"

"Certainly, towards the end of the quarter his pockets are always to let."

Everyone paused to admire a new fountain none of them had seen before, situated prettily beneath an arbour. Lavinia was deep in thought, disturbed by what Lord Ratcliffe had told her, although she could not quite understand why. Promissory notes were often exchanged between young men who invariably spent (or lost at gambling) an entire three months allowance in one week, but somehow it did not seem quite right in this instance.

"Lavinia is quiet tonight," Hattie whispered to Kitty Stapleton as they moved on again.

"She has the look of a moon-calf about her," the girl replied.

"Since last night!" the other gasped in wonder. "It cannot be Heathbury who is the cause."

"Who else? Cheriton never made her look so moonstruck. I think Lavinia has thrown her cap over the windmill at last. It is not before time either."

The girls were whispering between themselves and Lavinia was not certain it was intended for her to hear, but nevertheless she did and fear stabbed at her heart. She could not bear to have her most private and precious feelings bandied about in this way.

"It will be famous watching how matters develop," Hattie said gleefully, "especially as Heathbury and Cheriton are cousins. Quite ironic, isn't it, if she is in love with him now after all she said about him at Ardsley?"

"Should we not return to the box?" Lavinia suggested hastily. "It must almost be time for supper."

"Splendid idea," Lord Cheriton agreed, "I am dev'lish hungry."

"You are always hungry," Hattie teased and Lavinia drew a sigh of relief.

As they walked back to the Rotunda along a pleasant walk with the sound of music drifting across the talk and laughter, they passed a couple close in a passionate embrace. Many such assignations took place at Vauxhall between young lovers and also fashionable bucks and low harlots too. Lavinia invariably averted her eyes whenever she saw them, but on this occasion she looked at them curiously, wondering what it was to be kissed so thoroughly that nothing and no one else in the world mattered.

"Last night Lady Fairfield was promising that her ball next month will outshine Heathbury's although the plans for it are a secret," Kitty observed.

"I cannot conceive how she will achieve anything better," Lavinia answered.

"Perhaps she intends to have a river of claret and Buonaparte as guest of honour," Sir Christopher suggested to everyone's amusement.

They were still laughing when they arrived back at the Rotunda. Inevitably Lavinia looked immediately to see if the Earl had yet arrived and almost at once she stiffened. Suddenly the sky rocked above her as did the ground beneath her feet. Emotion rose in her throat and threatened to choke her. She wished she were a thousand miles away, in Newgate even, or in Bedlam where the inmates threw themselves around the floor in mental anguish as she had witnessed one day when she had joined a party visiting the asylum. She just wished she were anywhere but here, wanting to die there on the spot but pride ensuring that a smile was on her lips and her head remained high.

Lord Heathbury had arrived at last, but he was not in his uncle's box awaiting Lavinia's return with adoring looks and extravagant praise. He was standing in the centre of the Rotunda for all to see, talking and laughing with his *chère amie*, Mrs Byefield.

"Well," Hattie said resignedly, "I own that is a lesson to us all, ladies. Never take Lord Heathbury's attentions seriously."

At this Lavinia rounded on her. "I cannot conceive of anyone who would do so, except perhaps for you, Hattie."

With head held high she walked purposefully to the Duke's box where supper was about to be served. It was, however, another matter to be able to eat it. She felt quite ill with every mouthful but nevertheless pride and anger ensured that she forked it in to her mouth in an effort to preserve an air of normalcy. It was merciful that their party was a large one and her quietness could go almost unnoticed—for a while at least. From that moment onwards, though, the evening was going to seem endless. The jugglers and magician performing for their entertainment went unnoticed by Lavinia. She had sunk into a mire of longing and misery that nothing could relieve.

They had almost finished supper, with Lavinia refusing second helpings of any of the junkets and creams, when she caught sight of the Earl approaching the box. Immediately she was assailed by panic. She could not face him, having realised the truth of her feelings at last. Certainly she could not face him now when she felt so thoroughly humiliated; perhaps not ever.

He would look at her mockingly with everyone else attending her humiliation closely so they could report it to others not present. No doubt it was precisely what he planned but Lavinia was determined not to facilitate him. Just at that moment she felt she would suffocate, for she could not bear to be witness to his mockery, and worse, his indifference.

"Lavinia, are you unwell?" Lord Cheriton asked.

His question caused her to look at him in alarm, aware all the time that Lord Heathbury had paused to speak with an acquaintance.

"A slight headache only," she answered after a pause. "There is no need for alarm."

He continued to look concerned. "I thought that might be the case. In my opinion you have not been well since we arrived and I am well aware of the reason; you did drink a deal of champagne last night, to which you are not accustomed."

She gave him a wan smile, grateful for his concern. "I fear you are correct."

"I had better ask Mama to give you her vinaigrette."

He moved towards his mother who was engaged in a game of faro and as he did so Lavinia put a restraining hand on his arm. "Please don't, Theo. Everyone is enjoying themselves so much I am most reluctant to spoil it for them. It was wrong of me to come tonight, for I have had the headache all day. Only allow me to slip away quietly; I shall return home and have an early night for once. 'Tis all I really need and by the morrow I shall be quite recovered."

He pushed back his chair. "I am in full agreement that you should return home. Allow me to escort you to the carriage."

"Don't trouble, Theo. I would not for anything have everyone know I am indisposed."

"Then I must insist upon having the carriage brought round for you. Wait here for me. I will be but a few minutes."

Before she had a chance to argue further he had gone. Her head was truly throbbing now, so it was no Banbury Tale she had told him. She felt wretched, watching that handsome figure blandly conversing with a matron who was, if the expression on her face was anything by which to judge, utterly charmed by his manner. After a few minutes he made a slight bow and then continued towards his uncle's box. Panic began to rise in Lavinia's breast again and she got to her feet, slipping unseen out of the box. She drew her cloak about her and made her way quickly to where the carriage would wait.

She was half way along the walk when she hesitated, having detected echoing footsteps in her wake. When she paused, she glanced behind her to discover that it was the Earl who had been following her and he waited only a few yards away.

"Miss Merridew—Lavinia," he called and she was undecided whether to wait or hurry on. In any event he was too close now to be evaded. "I suspected it was you," he said, frowning slightly. "What the devil are you doing here alone? It is most unwise."

"I take leave to doubt your authority in questioning me, Lord Heathbury, but it so happens I am returning home. Your cousin is being kind enough to summon the carriage."

"Home? So early?"

"I have the headache." He took a step nearer and she added quickly, "I beseech you not to come too close; the headache may be the symptom of something far more serious. A pestilence of great virulence, perhaps."

He smiled then and did not heed her warning. "I am devastated that you are leaving so early. Since rising this morning I have scarce thought of anything save encountering you tonight."

Her lips curved into the semblance of a smile. "Whilst you are here making pretty, worthless speeches to me Mrs Byefield must be wondering where you are. You must not keep her waiting any longer."

His eyes opened wide in surprise. "She is doing no such thing. She has a party of friends in her box sufficient to divert her I think. She is an old acquaintance but I met her only by chance tonight on my way to my uncle's box."

Lavinia gave him a disbelieving look before turning away. It was not easy to walk away from him but as she did so he caught her by the arm, drawing her back towards him. When she looked up into his face she saw an expression of wonder on it.

"By all that's famous, you are jealous!"

"Of that kind of woman, Lord Heathbury? You insult me."

"No, little bird, I would not do that and you must not scorn women of her kind; they could teach chits like you a great many matters of importance."

"No doubt," she snapped and would have turned away again, this time to hide the tears which had come unbidden to her eyes, only he would not let her go.

174

As he drew her closer still she looked up at him through tear-filled eyes, only too well aware of the dangerous power he wielded over her. Accustomed to the power she normally held over men's hearts, it was a strange paradox and a heady one. Her head began to swim and the ground felt unsteady beneath her feet.

He looked down into her face, saying, "You have no rivals, for you must be the most beautiful woman in the world, Lavinia."

When he drew her closer still she had no will to resist, for it was only pride which tempted her to do so. His fingers gently brushed away a wispy curl which had come free of its pins and then a tear which had spilled on to her cheek. Then they touched her lips which waited for his kiss.

When he did kiss her she surrendered her lips to him as easily as she had given her heart. For so long she had wondered what it was like to be kissed; of late it was thoughts of being kissed by this man which had filled her mind. Now it had happened and it was more wonderful than any dream.

Breathless, at last he let her go and when she looked up at him her eyes were shining with newly-discovered adoration. "I love you,

Damien," she whispered and he kissed her again.

"I have never been able to make that admission to anyone before, but now I mean it with all my heart."

He looked at her for a long moment before drawing away. "Love? Do you really know what love is, Lavinia?"

She laughed but it was tinged with uncertainty. "You must know that I do."

"I think not. Love is just another game that is played by all. I might have been a trifle slow in learning the rules but now that I have do you not think I played it well?"

His smile was now a cruel one and Lavinia stared at him in horror. "No!" she cried. "You don't mean that. You cannot be serious."

But as she continued to gaze at him in disbelief she knew very well that it was true. All the tenderness and charm he had shown her was gone now, leaving only coldness and dislike. It was almost unbearable.

He turned on his heel and strode back towards the Rotunda. Lavinia watched him helplessly until the darkness had swallowed him up, and then the full horror of what had happened finally revealed itself to her.

This was his revenge. He had planned it

all the while and was only now complete; he had taken her affection from his cousin, stolen her heart and even controlled the purse strings of the other men he considered guilty of humiliating him.

Tears began to stream down her cheeks and she clutched her arms about her as if in pain. One or two passers by glanced at her strangely but she was beyond caring. All that mattered was her anguish, the pain of which there was no end.

It was in this situation that Lord Cheriton found her some minutes later. "Lavinia," he said in a censorious tone, "you should not be here. Did I not tell you to wait in the box? Good grief!" he cried when he saw her distress. "My dear, you *are* ill. Come, we must get you home."

"Oh yes, Theo. Please take me home."

"The carriage is nearby so there is not far to walk." He put a helping arm around her and she was glad enough to allow him to take her weight. "A physician will have to be called immediately. I had no notion you were so wretched."

"No, no," she protested. "There must be no fuss. I just wish to go to bed and rest."

"And that is just what you shall do," he

said soothingly and his tone of voice was sufficient to cause tears to well up in her eyes once more. If only, she thought in anguish, the love of her life had been destined to be he.

He looked so concerned as he was about to hand her into the carriage that her misery deepened. She sank back into the squabs wearily, hardly able to comprehend that a man who could kiss her so passionately did so with hate in his heart.

Lord Cheriton was still looking at her worriedly. "I feel that someone should accompany you, Lavinia."

Suddenly she sat forward. "Theo, do you think me a wicked woman?"

Quite naturally he looked shocked. "You are the epitome of goodness."

"And do you wish to marry me still?" she asked in a harsh whisper.

"Oh, Lavinia, you know I do. Tomorrow if it were at all possible."

"If only it were!" she cried from the heart.

"Lavinia, are you in earnest?"

"Our betrothal can be announced as soon as my brother-in-law thinks fit."

The pleasure evident on his face was

reward enough, far more than she felt she deserved.

"My dearest love, I have been waiting for this moment for an eternity. You will never regret entrusting yourself to me."

"I know that, Theo," she answered in a choked voice.

"Now," he went on, taking her hand in his, "We may talk of this when you are more robust. Home with you."

She sank back in the squabs and waved to him briefly as the carriage set off. Then she closed her eyes wearily. She could only truly love one man and he had rejected her most cruelly. Now she was determined to devote her life to making Theo happy. If she should live to be a hundred years old she would never knowingly hurt another person as she had hurt the Earl, for the price of doing so was far too high.

Eleven

"If Madame will only stand still, the fitting will be complete in one minute." The mantua-maker's voice was growing more shrill with her mounting frustration.

"I cannot stand still another moment," Lavinia complained. "You will have to come back another day; I am too tired to continue any longer with this."

So saying, she stood down and her maid, Phoebe, rushed forward to unhook the bridal gown of parchment silk embroidered with diamonte and ribbons. As she did so Lavinia caught sight of her reflection in a mirror. Her face was drawn with strain and although the gown was magnificent she was quick to struggle out of it.

The mantua-maker tut-tutted about not being able to have the gown ready on time if she did not receive cooperation, but Lavinia did not heed her. Phoebe continued to hook her into her day dress.

The mantua-maker's assistant folded the wedding gown and collected together all her employer's belongings whilst Phoebe fussed around Lavinia's hair, tucking in all escaping curls.

"I will return on Thursday, Madame," the woman informed her before sweeping out of the room.

Lavinia drew a sigh of relief and Phoebe continued to tidy her hair. "You will make the most beautiful bride, ma'am."

"Thank you, Phoebe," she answered in a muted tone. "You may go now. I shall not require you again this morning."

Before leaving the room she looked at her mistress worriedly. "You haven't got the headache again, ma'am?"

Lavinia smiled wanly. "No, Phoebe, I am perfectly all right. All I require is a little peace and quiet."

"I know what you mean ma'am. Life is growing quite hectic and I fear we'll all be fit for Bedlam by the time it is over."

"I shall be a prime contender for that institution," Lavinia thought to herself as Phoebe left the room, only to be replaced moments later by Elizabeth.

"I have just met Madame Grimond, Lavinia, and she appears to be in high dudgeon. She says you are in a constant fidge whenever she tries to fit your gown."

"Oh, that woman is so infuriating," Lavinia complained, venting her frustration on the absent woman. "Why can she not understand any normal human being is unable to stand still for hours on end."

"Surely it is not as bad as that, dearest."

Lavinia's face relaxed into a smile as she gazed at her now slim sister. "Of course not. I am being needlessly peevish, that is all. You must not mind me."

"Every prospective bride feels as you do as the wedding day approaches. I recall the feeling well."

Lavinia was glad to have her feelings

explained away with such ease and some of her tension faded then. "Is she truly Madame Grimond of Paris? Her accent seems exceedingly strange to me."

Elizabeth laughed, "I am reliably informed that she is really a Mrs Grimsdyke but she feels a French name and accent beneficial to her craft. She is very much in demand so we should humour her a little."

"Tush. The honour is hers. Mine is the wedding of the year, is it not? Our patronage can do her nothing but good so it is she who should be humouring me."

All the while she had been speaking her sister had been gazing at her in an appraising way. "Lavinia, you do look a trifle peaked. Perhaps you are indulging in too much activity. You are forever in a fidge; I have noted it myself."

Lavinia forced a smile to her face. "This, dear Eliza, is my first and last Season as a debutante and I intend to enjoy it to the full."

"Your last fling as it were."

"Precisely."

"But you once declared that life would remain exciting even after you married."

A shadow crossed Lavinia's face before she

replied brightly, "Oh, that was romantic nonsense. Next Season I shall be a staid married woman with an establishment of my own just like you, Eliza."

Elizabeth laughed and yet her eyes still reflected her disquiet. "Impudence." And then she suggested, "Why don't you go out and take some air, dearest? The weather is most clement and I am sure an airing will be beneficial to you."

"That is precisely what I intended to do. I need some lace and buttons, and want to change my book at the circulating library in Bond Street."

"You seem to be reading a great deal nowadays."

The shadow once again passed across Lavinia's face before she answered brightly, "It is a pursuit I have learned to enjoy."

"You must take care not to become a bluestocking. Cheriton would not like that. He prefers you to be light-hearted."

"I know," Lavinia answered wistfully and then smiling at her sister, "I shall take care to heed your warning."

As she went towards the door Elizabeth said in a thoughtful voice, "Lady Durrant was saying, when she visited me yesterday, how odd it seemed that Lord Heathbury hasn't been seen in Town of late. It seems he has vanished entirely."

Lavinia's hand was on the doorknob but now she hesitated before saying in a voice devoid of all emotion, "Theo informs me his cousin had to depart for Norfolk to attend to matters of estate business."

"But how odd that is. He was so enjoying every diversion one would imagine he might postpone it until the end of the Season which is not so far hence."

"I was given to understand the matter was an urgent one."

"Well, no doubt he will return to be present at your wedding."

The knowledge stabbed at Lavinia's heart. Of course he would be there; apart from the fact that he was Lord Cheriton's cousin, more to the point he would not miss this opportunity to gloat on the success of his revenge.

Once again she forced a bright smile to her face. "How is little Matthew this morning?"

Fortunately Lavinia knew that her sister was easily diverted by mention of her baby son. "He is sleeping now, the little lamb. It is wonderful how good he is, content just to eat and sleep."

Lavinia chuckled. "Make the most of that, Eliza. I'll warrant he will soon demand much more attention."

"Walter cannot wait to put him on a horse. He is quite frustrated at having to wait.

"If you are indeed going to shop you had best go now," she added quickly, "but before you go you might like to inspect the latest gifts to arrive. Lord Ratcliffe has sent a silver epergne which is quite magnificent. In view of his unsuccessful suit I regard it as exceeding generous."

Lavinia went immediately to the ballroom where the gifts were being displayed—hers and Theo's. Silver-gilt, crystal, rare marbles abounded everywhere but Lavinia viewed them through mist-shrouded eyes. Her heart ached unbearably at a time when it should have been soaring with happiness.

After a few moments she ran out of the ballroom, panicking in a way which occurred often of late whenever left to her own thoughts, invariably of the Earl. She knew she should hate him, but love, she recognized, did not reason, for she did love him as much as ever.

She paused outside the ballroom, drawing a deep sigh. If only she had envisaged what an ordeal this wedding was going to be she might never have embarked on the betrothal. She would have gladly married Theo quickly and quietly after the cruel rejection by Lord Heathbury, but the pomp and panoply people had attached to what some were calling the wedding of the year, only served to increase the emptiness in her heart. Not that she feared failing the man she was going to marry, or even cheating him. She still loved him as she had always done and had vowed never to let him discover he was not the love of her life.

Spring was well-advanced. Fruit trees had long since burgeoned into bloom and were now casting their blossom onto garden paths which looked as though they were covered with fragrant snow.

The wedding date had been set to take place just before the King's birthday which signalled the end of the Season. After the wedding the newly-weds would be travelling to Scotland where Lord Cheriton had a beautiful estate and they would stay the summer.

As Lavinia sat alone, for once, on a seat in an arbour in the garden of her sister's home she reflected that the long-awaited Season had not turned out quite as she had expected. Throughout her life she had been determined to marry only the man she loved to distraction and as there was no one in the family likely to thwart her, it seemed that is just what she would do. The problem was that she had fallen in love with the wrong man. The fact that she had thrown away a perfectly good chance of winning his devotion was like a bitter potion she was forced to swallow at frequent intervals.

She glanced down at the book she had been attempting to read—an English translation of Pliny. She was experiencing very little success in understanding it, but some strange whim had induced her to borrow it from the library, blushing as the proprietor had looked at her in astonishment. Hopefully no one of her acquaintance would see her reading it, for she would be at a total loss how to explain her interest.

Not far away the garden gate closed with a loud snap, causing her to close the book. That particular entrance was rarely used, except perhaps by servants seeking to steal a little time for private business.

"This time next week I shall be wed," she thought to herself, refusing even to consider what her feelings might have been now if the Earl was to be her bridegroom. Thinking in such terms was not only unfair to Theo but caused her needless anguish too.

Ever since that disastrous evening at Vauxhall, Lavinia had filled her days and evenings with as much activity as she could manage in an effort to blot out the pain, and as a ploy it was reasonably successful. If on some nights she remained awake dreaming of what might have been there was no one to know of it.

Footsteps on the gravelled path close at hand caused her to look up in alarm and her heart almost stopped beating at the sight of the person standing a few paces away. Hope and love leapt like a flame in her breast only to be replaced seconds later by resentment.

"What are you doing here?" she demanded, jumping to her feet and fighting back the panic that assailed her. Instinctively she glanced behind her for a means of retreat. When she returned her frightened gaze to him she realised the cynical look, the coldness in his manner, was no longer apparent.

The Earl looked quite diffident and although he was dressed in the height of elegance and fashion which she had come to expect of him, Lavinia was immediately reminded of the time when she first knew him at Ardsley.

"I am sorry if I startled you," he said after a moment.

"I certainly did not look to see anyone in this part of the garden, much less you, Lord Heathbury."

"My apologies then for the intrusion, Miss Merridew, but I particularly wished to speak with you alone. When I called on your sister it was mentioned that you were here and on leaving I decided to take the liberty of seeking you out."

She turned on her heel lest he should notice the mixture of agony and joy on her face. "Lord Heathbury, I am persuaded enough was said on our last encounter."

"Oh yes indeed," he answered bitterly, "more than enough. That is why I am here— to entreat your forgiveness."

At this she turned to face him once more, her hands clasped together in front of her to still their trembling. "That is indeed magnanimous of you, considering you were in some way justified."

He stared at the ground, or rather his highly polished hessians. "I am afraid my reaction to what was only a jest was extreme in its severity."

Lavinia drew a sharp breath. "Well, we are equal now, are we not? 'Tis an abject lesson not to fool with human emotions."

"You are very generous, Miss Merridew," he told her, still not looking at her directly.

"Not at all. It was noble of you to wish to apologise."

"I have," he went on with noticeable effort, "congratulated my cousin on his good fortune, and all that remains now is for me to wish you happy."

Tears sparkled in Lavinia's eyes and she fought them back as she held out her hand to him. "Thank you, Lord Heathbury."

He looked at her at last and she was forced to swallow a lump which had formed in her throat. She hoped above hope he would go now lest she broke down in front of him. The encounter did not augur well for the times she would be obliged to meet him in the future.

With some reluctance he touched her proffered hand briefly. She watched him turn away, but as he did so he caught sight of the book which she had pushed to the back of the seat. Her heart skipped a beat as he paused to examine it briefly before straightening up and looking at her curiously. Once more she was forced to avert her eyes.

"Lavinia, I simply cannot go without asking the question which has been plaguing me for weeks. Did you mean what you said that night at Vauxhall? Were your feelings really true?"

"What was said all those weeks ago can have no relevance now," she murmured.

He flung his curly-brimmed beaver onto the seat and clutched her by both arms. "By jove, I shall not go until I have my answer!" Still she remained silent. "I must know," he insisted. "You cannot marry him; I shall not let you."

"You can do nothing to stop me, Lord Heathbury, and I beg of you to let me go. This behaviour is unwarranted."

"Lavinia," he said in a pleading tone which smote her heart, "I am in torment. Can you not see that?"

"No more than I!" she cried silently.

He put one hand beneath her chin and turned her face to his. Tears trembled on her lashes and her lips quivered with the emotion she could no longer control.

"In seeking to punish you, I have only succeeded in putting myself in torment. Can you not see that? I love you, Lavinia, more than life itself and have done since the day you came into the library at Ardsley and brought this heart to life for the first time. That passion fed the need to revenge myself on you, but I have gained no satisfaction. If it is true you love me then I have perpetrated the most dreadful crime in rejecting you. No fleeting blow for my pride is worth the anguish I have suffered since, and like to endure for the rest of my days."

The tears spilled over onto her cheeks as she threw herself into his arms at last, clinging on to him tightly. "You must know I spoke from the heart."

With great tenderness he kissed the tears from her cheeks. "I believe I knew, but I was too proud to acknowledge it. Bitterness only allowed room for the need to revenge myself."

He drew her down on to the seat, kissing her all the while. Lavinia felt as though she had been dead for an eternity and only now became gloriously alive.

At last she drew away from him, breathless and laughing. "You were so diabolically clever, Damien. I suspected all along you harboured a grudge against me, but I never dreamed you intended such revenge against us all."

For a moment he looked troubled. "Diabolical perhaps, but not clever, Lavinia, and I wish you would not remind me of my folly."

"From today it is quite forgotten."

He kissed her hand longingly until his lips reached the heirloom ring Lord Cheriton had given her on the occasion of their betrothal.

"You do recognise that you will be obliged to cancel this wedding now. It cannot possibly take place."

Suddenly Lavinia's eyes filled with horror for in her happiness she had entirely forgotten Theo, but before she could reply he went on, "You need have no fear, my love, I shall speak with your brother-in-law, and I know I can make my cousin understand. He is most reasonable I believe . . ."

She withdrew her hands from his grasp and folded them in her lap. "No, Damien, you must not on any account approach them."

"I have no intention of allowing you to face this ordeal on your own. It is for me to put matters to rights, and without further delay."

"No!" she cried in anguish. "You do not understand. Neither of us will tell them. It is too late!"

His brow furrowed slightly. "Too late? It is not that until next Friday."

She shook her head, not daring to look at him for fear of losing her resolve. "The wedding must go ahead as planned. I cannot countenance any other course."

"No, Lavinia! You cannot mean to marry him, not *now*."

"I must. I am promised to him." She twisted her hands together in her lap. "It was *my* decision to marry Theo. No one arranged it, or forced me to accept him against my will."

"But it was my behaviour which drove you to him!"

"That is of no consequence."

He caught hold of her again, roughly this time and she could not bear to witness his distress which equalled her own. "I love you, Lavinia! And what is more important, you love me. You couldn't possibly be happy with my cousin."

"Nor could I be happy without him now, I fear."

Furious and frustrated he turned away from her. "I cannot believe such madness exists."

She held out her hands to him beseechingly. "Oh, please understand, Damien! I cannot ruin Theo's happiness now. Surely you of all people can understand why. And there is your aunt and uncle to consider; they have hoped for this match for so long. I have to consider my own family too; my sister is still weak from child-bed. Oh, Damien, my love, I cannot humiliate them!"

"And I cannot accept what you are saying."

Gently she told him, "If you truly love me you will; I do not do this lightly, for I shall never love another as I love you."

His answering sigh was a profound one. "If you are determined on this course, one thing is quite certain; I shall not remain in this country to see you as his wife. I *cannot* remain here and see you by his side, bearing his children . . ."

"What shall you do?" she asked him in a whisper.

"I shall go back to Jamaica, I think. It will be the best course for both our sakes."

She bowed her head in misery and then with sudden ferocity he pulled her into his arms once more. Knowing it was the last time, Lavinia had neither the will nor the wish to resist. His kisses now were rough and demanding, and although they were possibly bruising too she responded wholeheartedly.

"Hell and damnation! What the devil is going on here?"

The angry voice brought them back to reality with a start. Both she and the Earl jumped to their feet, Lavinia quickly smoothing back her dishevelled curls and straightening her crumpled gown.

"Theo," she said in a voice which was shaking with emotion, "we did not hear your approach."

Lord Cheriton's eyes blazed with fury as they surveyed first Lavinia and then Lord Heathbury. Lavinia had rarely seen him so angry in all their long years' acquaintance.

"I'll warrant you did not."

Lord Heathbury stepped forward. "Cheriton, allow me to explain . . ."

The young man rounded on him furiously.

198

"No, by jove I will not. You will meet me over this, Heathbury. I demand satisfaction."

"Oh no!" Lavinia cried. "I beseech you . . ."

Lord Heathbury laughed uncertainly. "Cheriton, there is no need for me to meet you over this."

"So, you treat it lightly, but let me remind you my future wife is no lightskirt to be accosted where you will."

The Earl's eyes grew hard. "I am well aware of her worth—perhaps more than even you. Nonetheless, I have no wish to fight you."

Lord Cheriton's lips curved into the travesty of a smile. "You are a cowardly worm, Heathbury, despite your top-lofty ways, and I always knew it was so."

At this the Earl thumped his fist down on the back of the garden seat. "No man calls me a coward! I will meet you, Cheriton, on your terms too. Name the place, weapons and your seconds as soon as you please."

He snatched up his hat and would have gone quickly, only he paused to give Lavinia one last look. She could only gaze back at him imploringly and then he hurried back the way he had come. She was on the point of following but at that moment Lord Cheriton started back down the path towards the house.

"Theo! Don't go! Please don't go just yet."

Because he did not slow his pace she had to run to keep up with him. "We have nothing to say to each other, Lavinia, until this matter is resolved."

"You cannot mean to proceed with this duel."

"I most certainly do."

"But you might be killed!"

"Then the best man will have won."

"I cannot allow you to duel over me. It is too ludicrous."

He paused by the house door. "Lavinia, it is a matter of honour between gentlemen and you must not interfere."

"You are duelling over me, so I must have some rights in this matter!"

"No," he answered gently.

"Oh, Theo, please see sense. If neither of you will behave sensibly I shall be forced to inform the authorities and that is most certain to put an end to this folly."

He gave her a crooked smile. "You would not dare. Would you see us rot in jail instead?"

She covered her face with her hands. "It

was nothing. You must believe you are making something out of nothing."

He pulled her hands away from her face so that she was forced to look at him. "You are a scheming minx, Lavinia, and I only wonder I never saw it in you before."

"It isn't true, Theo. This meeting was an accidental one, the kiss merely a moment's aberration. Would you blight all our lives for ever because of it?"

"I am no green boy, Lavinia. If I believe for one second it was a moment's aberration I would have ignored the matter entirely, but how can you claim it meant nothing? You were kissing each other with a passion which defied all reason."

At so faithful an observation she could find nothing more to say and sank back against the door which he had thrown back, numb and shocked. He left her there, drained of all emotion although she knew the pain would soon begin anew.

"Theo," she called weakly, but it was to no avail. He had gone.

Twelve

"Duel? Good grief, I thought Cheriton far too sensible to indulge in such nonsense."

Walter Lovell almost choked over his favourite pigeon pie. "And Heathbury, of all men. Wasn't he that bookish fellow? It seems exceeding cork-brained of them."

"Dearest," his wife crooned, "I beseech you not to get into a pucker over this."

Lavinia, pale and wan, simply stared at her plate where food remained uneaten.

"Cheriton and Heathbury duelling," he went on. "Over what, I ask you?"

Lavinia said nothing. She was grateful at least that her sister and brother-in-law did not yet know the reason for the duel, although that was only a short respite she didn't doubt.

"Over something quite trivial, I don't doubt," Elizabeth answered, glancing worriedly at her sister. "And I would be obliged if you would not discuss it any further for now. Naturally Lavinia is distressed, and of course they will be in great trouble if word of this should get out."

Walter chuckled as he helped himself to more pie and indicated to the footman to pour him more wine. "The word must be out already if *you* have heard of it, my love. And if not, the entire world will know of it by tomorrow. It is too bad of Cheriton. The wedding is only a week away; what if he should be injured—or even killed."

Lavinia could bear no more. She pushed back her chair and, murmuring, "Excuse me," she hurried from the room.

"There, look what you have done," Elizabeth complained. "I wish you would not be so insensitive, Walter. It is quite evident that the girl is in a torment."

He looked up worriedly before grunting and applying himself to his food once more. "No doubt then the chit will not feel much like attending the Fortesque's rout this evening."

"No, she will not! And, Walter Lovell, let me tell you, neither shall we!"

Lavinia ran swiftly up the stairs, brushing away a tear. Phoebe, who was still tidying her mistress's room, looked surprised to see her returned so soon.

"Phoebe, did you deliver my note to Lord Cheriton?"

"Yes ma'am, just as you directed into his hands personally. Not that His Lordship's butler was pleased to let me, but I was not about to go until I had and he could see my determination."

"And the reply?" she asked eagerly.

"None, ma'am. Said to tell you there was none, but that he would see you for breakfast in the morning."

Lavinia twisted her hands in anguish before asking breathlessly, "And the one you delivered to Lord Heathbury?"

"He wasn't at his lodgings, ma'am, so I thought I'd go along to his house in the event he'd called in there, but it was to no avail. Would you have me return and wait for him?"

She gave the woman a faint smile and shook her head. "You have tried your best, Phoebe, and I thank you."

"I just wish I could do more to help, ma'am. It torments me to see you fretting yourself like this. What to do next?"

Lavinia sank down onto the bed, staring morosely at the carpet, its pattern blurring before her eyes. "Nothing. There is nothing more I can do. They are intent upon destroying each other."

"It may not be so bad. They do not have to kill or maim."

"They will. It goes far deeper than what happened here yesterday. I realise that now."

"Well, you would be foolish to fret on it further, ma'am. You must rest now, otherwise you will be utterly ruined by the morrow."

At this observation Lavinia was forced to laugh brokenly. "No doubt."

"Not in that sense, ma'am," Phoebe answered, setting out Lavinia's bed gown.

"I shall be notorious, won't I, having two

gentlemen duelling over me? What Elizabeth will think when she discovers the truth of the matter I dare not imagine. Oh, Theo is such a good shot."

Lavinia was not obliged to wonder about her sister's thoughts for much longer. At that moment her bedroom door opened and Elizabeth herself, lighted by the candle she held, came in.

"Dearest, I must have words with you," she said immediately, causing her sister to quail.

She came quickly across the room and sat down next to Lavinia on the bed. "You do know what this duel is about, don't you?" Lavinia averted her face and Elizabeth went on, "Is it over you?" When she did not answer Elizabeth sighed. "I feared as much. No doubt Walter will hear of it the moment he steps out tomorrow, but at least by then it will be over."

Lavinia covered her face with her hands which shook convulsively with emotion. "Oh, Eliza, I am so miserable."

"I don't doubt that you are," she said gently, "but that is a useless emotion. You must consider what you will do afterwards. Which of them do you favour?"

Lavinia looked at her in astonishment. "How can you be so matter of fact over this?"

Her sister smiled faintly. "Young men are invariably hotheads and there is nothing we females can do to stop them being so."

"Damien . . . Heathbury is not a hothead."

Elizabeth put a comforting hand over her sister's. "Is it he you truly love, dearest?" She nodded mutely and her sister sighed once more. "In that event you must wait and hope."

"I cannot hope that he kills Theo!"

"Lavinia you must put all such thoughts from your mind. Whatever transpires on the morrow remember always that you are blameless."

At this Lavinia threw back her head and laughed, laughter tinged with hysteria. In much alarm Elizabeth got to her feet, retreating quickly. "I think I will leave you to Phoebe's ministrations. You are obviously overwrought and cannot think properly." She looked anxiously to the maid. "Make her a posset, Phoebe, and then make certain she goes to bed."

"Yes, ma'am. That is just what I intended to do."

Just as her sister was about to leave the

room, Lavinia said, "I am sorry, Eliza. I did not wish this to happen."

Elizabeth paused to give a faint smile. "I know, dearest."

As soon as the door had closed behind her Phoebe drew her to her feet and soon had her in her bedgown. Over it she slipped a silk peignoir of oyster satin, like so many similar garments collected for her trousseau.

"Come to the dressing table, ma'am, and I will remove the pins from your hair."

Like a child Lavinia did as she was bid, but a few moments later said, "There must be a way to stop them, Phoebe. There must."

"No, ma'am, there is none. Nothing you can do will make one bit of difference. You might just as well try to put a hat on a hen."

Lavinia stared at her pale reflection in the mirror and sighed, knowing it to be true, but the thought of either of these men being hurt—or worse—tore at her heart.

Two candles burned low in sconces at each side of the dressing table mirror. Every time Lavinia paced to and fro she caught sight of herself reflected there, a wraith with no substance. It was tempting to snuff those candles, but the dark was no friend in her present state of mind. The coming dawn held even more terrors.

A light tap on the door caused her to start, and then moments later Phoebe entered the room, lightening it immediately with the candle she held aloft in one hand.

"Ma'am you should not be out of your bed."

"I could not sleep, Phoebe, however hard I tried."

"Oh, ma'am, you'll catch your death out of bed. See, I have brought you chocolate."

"That is very kind of you, Phoebe, but you should not yet be abroad."

"I knew you'd be up and fretting, and doing yourself no good at all. Here, drink the chocolate and perchance you'll sleep 'til noon."

Lavinia laughed harshly. "There is no possibility of my doing so and well you know it." She made no attempt to drink the chocolate and as the maid tried to revive the embers of the fire, Lavinia said, "Leave that, Phoebe, and choose me a warm gown."

"You have no intention of rising now, ma'am, surely."

"I must take this one last opportunity of trying to halt this madness. I'll wear my winter cloak too, the one with the sable lining."

"But it is not yet dawn!" the maid protested.

"Phoebe, do as I bid you."

When she looked at her mistress she could see that her panic had gone and only resolve was left in its place. "Yes, ma'am," she answered meekly, hurrying to the press, "although what Mrs Lovell will say I don't care to think about."

"We shall ponder on that in the morning. Here, help me out of this bedgown."

A few minutes later Lavinia was warmly gowned and as Phoebe slipped her cloak over her shoulders, she ordered, "Go quickly and have a carriage brought round. It matters not which one as long as it will travel."

"Oh, ma'am, are you quite decided to go?"

Lavinia stared into space. "I have spent the entire night thinking of nothing else. I have no choice. Please go now, Phoebe, lest we are too late."

A few minutes later a sleepy-eyed footman was handing her into one of her brother-in-law's town carriages to make the short journey to Hyde Park where the duel was to take place at daybreak. The driver looked phlegmatic at being roused from his bed earlier than usual; servants were used to the strange whims of their aristocratic masters.

"Oh, do hurry," Lavinia urged, biting her lip anxiously.

The roads were not as empty as she would have hoped. Tradesmen's drays were already abroad, delivering fresh supplies to the shops. At last, however, the carriage sped into the Park and Lavinia then put her head out of the window ready to spot the illicit gathering the moment it came into sight.

The cool morning breeze blew the hood from her head, revealing her undressed hair which flew back from her face.

"Ma'am, you will become chilled, indeed you will," Phoebe warned. "Come back inside."

"I can see their carriages! Over there, Frensham. Quickly!"

The driver flicked his whip over the backs of the team of horses and they ploughed across the fields, startling the cattle already grazing there.

Lavinia did not wait for the footman to help her down. The moment the steps were lowered she dashed out and across to where the men were gathered. To one side the Earl was in conversation with his seconds and at a fair distance, Lord Cheriton and his seconds. A few yards away, isolated from the rest the surgeon waited, clutching his bag of instruments. Clad in black, he looked to Lavinia, who slowed her pace and shuddered, like a carrion crow awaiting to descend on its prey.

Before approaching anyone and aware of her unconventional behaviour in coming at all she looked to where the Earl was standing. He gazed back at her for a long moment and then turned away. The gesture cut her to the quick, but she made no move to approach him; it was Lord Cheriton she wished to see at that moment as he was the challenger, and she waited, hesitant now, as he marched purposefully towards her.

"Lavinia, are you mad to come here?"

"Yes, we are all mad to be here," she retorted, her eyes flashing fire.

"I insist that you leave immediately."

"Oh, Theo, there is still time to cry off."

He smiled grimly. "I have no intention of doing so."

"I know you were angry yesterday—and rightly so—but surely you have had time to ponder on it since."

"Oh, indeed," he answered in an uncharacteristically grim way, looking resolute. "You heard me call Heathbury a coward; I have no intention of giving him leave to level that accusation at *me*."

"Foolish pride is behind all this, nothing more. For my sake, Theo, please withdraw."

The grim smile was still on his face. "It is for your sake I fight this duel, Lavinia." As she averted her eyes, he added in a softer tone, "Whatever the outcome, remember that I love you."

"You cannot love me to cause me such anguish!"

He put one hand on her shoulder. "Lavinia, my dear, every one of your acquaintances would give a year's allowance to have a duel fought over them, so make the most of it."

Her head snapped up. "Your attic's to let if you believe I could enjoy any part of this. You're all mad. One of you might die! Oh, I cannot bear it."

Her voice was near to breaking as he answered, gently again, "Go away, Lavinia. This is between Heathbury and myself."

"Do not imagine I will marry the victor," she told him heatedly, "for I shall not."

He turned on his heel and in one last attempt to sway him she cried, "Recall he is your cousin."

Lord Cheriton glanced back at her, his

face cold and distant for once. "I would want to kill him even if he were my brother."

Tears misted her eyes once more and in desperation she ran across the field to where the Earl was standing, slightly apart from his seconds and apparently deep in thought. When she caught him by the arm and gave him an imploring look he started.

"Cheriton will not see sense, so *you* must cry off, Damien. He is a crack shot."

He smiled at her as she continued to clutch at his hand. "Such concern for me, Lavinia. Do you not concern yourself for Cheriton too?"

"Naturally I do. I cannot bear the thought of either of you being hurt—or worse, but he is such a good shot."

"Do you not think that I might be too?"

"If anything happens to either of you I shall not be able to live with the knowledge. I love you both."

The Earl's mocking smile disappeared. "That is sufficient reason for me to fight him."

"But only you have my heart, Damien. I promise I will go away with you, anywhere if only you will cry off."

Gently he disengaged her hand as his

seconds stepped forward. "I cannot. You must see that it would not answer."

As if stung she drew away from him. "Then I tell you what I told your cousin; whichever one of you is the victor shall not win me."

"Then we shall both lose, for it is over you we fight."

He signalled Phoebe to approach and when she did so he told her, "Take your mistress back home. This is no fit place for her."

Phoebe took hold of Lavinia who gave the Earl one last beseeching look before going with her maid. When she reached the carriage the driver and footmen were standing with arms folded, watching the proceedings with great relish. Glancing back she saw that the two men were selecting their weapons.

"I shall hate you both until eternity," she cried and then Phoebe tried to urge her into the carriage.

"Come now, ma'am, do as His Lordship wishes and go home. You can be of no help here."

"I cannot go," she answered tearfully. "Oh, Phoebe, Lord Cheriton was always such a good shot."

"Perhaps Lord Heathbury is too, ma'am."

"That is just as bad. They will kill each other."

The duellists were taking their places and Lavinia buried her face in Phoebe's shoulder. "I cannot watch them."

"I do wish you would go home, ma'am. You're like to take with a brain fever after all this fretting."

Suddenly two pistol shots cracked in the air, silencing the morning chorus and causing a host of birds to rise up from the trees all around. The horses snickered despite the groom's soothing hands, and the air was filled with the desperate beating of wings.

Lavinia shuddered convulsively at the sound and then Phoebe said, "It is all over, ma'am."

"Which . . . which one of them . . . is hurt?" she asked haltingly, her face still averted.

"Only see for yourself, ma'am, do."

Slowly and fearfully she raised her head, dreading what sight might meet her eyes. The surgeon was walking away from the scene and Lavinia had to blink twice before she could credit what she did see, for both combatants were still on their feet. She continued to cling on to Phoebe whilst she stared in astonishment, seeking any sign of blood or injury about their persons.

The coachman and footmen turned away in disgust, muttering between themselves at being cheated of a gory spectacle.

"Both their lordships fired into the air," Phoebe told her.

Lavinia's face broke into a smile of pure delight at last. "Oh, how wonderful!"

Lord Cheriton was handing his pistol to one of his seconds and the Earl was just staring at the ground, the pistol limp in his hand. Lavinia started forward but was not certain to which man she should go. As Lord Cheriton was being helped into his greatcoat he looked at her and she went towards him.

Tears were once again trembling on her lashes, tears of gladness this time. "Theo, I am so sorry about everything which has happened."

To her relief he smiled as he adjusted his neckcloth and smoothed a wrinkle from his coat. "Your presence effectively spoiled everything, Lavinia. I could not kill him with you looking on, and 'tis obvious he felt the same about me."

"You will never know how glad I am matters have worked out in this way."

Rachelle Edwards

His eyes took on a sudden sparkle. "I believe I do. Recall, I know you well."

"Do you still wish to marry me on Friday?" she asked breathlessly.

"Oh, yes," he breathed, "more than ever, but," he added, taking her hand in his, "I shall not be foolish enough to do so."

He raised her hand to his lips briefly before removing the betrothal ring from her finger. Lavinia looked at him questioningly as he said, "Tell my cousin that if he ever makes you unhappy, I will shoot to kill next time."

"Theo . . ." she began, the lump in her throat, making speech difficult.

"Just be happy, Lavinia, that is all I ask."

She had no further opportunity of saying anything more, for he turned on his heel and, beckoning to his seconds and servants, hurried to the waiting carriage. Lavinia remained where she was, watching him go, and then, after glancing to the Earl, who was being enrobed in his caped driving coat by a servant, she hesitated further.

She was uncertain that he still wanted her. After causing him so much unhappiness she would not blame him if he did not. He gazed across the expanse of field to her for

219

what seemed to be an eternity and then, sensing something in his attitude, she hesitated no longer.

Her heart soared with happiness as she ran towards him, to be enfolded in his arms immediately and they clung on to each other desperately for a long while until he began to kiss her, at first gently and then with growing passion. At last he drew away and they started to walk to the carriage together just as the sun was beginning to rise, heralding a new and beautiful dawn.

Let COVENTRY Give You
A Little Old-Fashioned Romance

CLASSIC BESTSELLERS
from FAWCETT BOOKS

ALL QUIET ON THE WESTERN FRONT by Erich Maria Remarque	23808	$2.25
TO KILL A MOCKINGBIRD by Harper Lee	08376	$1.95
SHOW BOAT by Edna Ferber	23191	$1.95
THEM by Joyce Carol Oates	23944	$2.50
THE FAMILY MOSKAT by Isaac Bashevis Singer	24066	$2.95
THE FLOUNDER by Gunter Grass	24180	$2.95
THE CHOSEN by Chaim Potok	24200	$2.50
NORTHWEST PASSAGE by Kenneth Roberts	02719	$2.50
THE CENTAUR by John Updike	22922	$1.75
JALNA by Mazo de la Roche	24118	$1.95
CENTENNIAL by James Michener	23494	$2.95

This offer expires 1 July 81   8400-1

A NEW DECADE OF
CREST BESTSELLERS

THE LAST ENCHANTMENT *Mary Stewart*	24207	$2.95
THE SPRING OF THE TIGER *Victoria Holt*	24297	$2.75
THE POWER EATERS *Diana Davenport*	24287	$2.75
A WALK ACROSS AMERICA *Peter Jenkins*	24277	$2.75
SUNFLOWER *Marilyn Sharp*	24269	$2.50
BRIGHT FLOWS THE RIVER		
Taylor Caldwell	24149	$2.95
CENTENNIAL *James A. Michener*	23494	$2.95
CHESAPEAKE *James A. Michener*	24163	$3.95
THE COUP *John Updike*	24259	$2.95
DRESS GRAY *Lucian K. Truscott IV.*	24158	$2.75
THE GLASS FLAME *Phyllis A. Whitney*	24130	$2.25
PRELUDE TO TERROR *Helen MacInnes*	24034	$2.50
SHOSHA *Isaac Bashevis Singer*	23997	$2.50
THE STORRINGTON PAPERS		
Dorothy Eden	24239	$2.50
THURSDAY THE RABBI WALKED OUT		
Harry Kemelman	24070	$2.25

Buy them at your local bookstore or use this handy coupon for ordering.

COLUMBIA BOOK SERVICE (a CBS Publications Co.)
32275 Mally Road, P.O. Box FB, Madison Heights, MI 48071

Please send me the books I have checked above. Orders for less than
5 books must include 75¢ for the first book and 25¢ for each addi-
tional book to cover postage and handling. Orders for 5 books or
more postage is FREE. Send check or money order only.

Cost $_____ Name _____

Postage_____ Address_____

Sales tax*_____ City_____

Total $_____ State_____ Zip_____

The government requires us to collect sales tax in all states except
AK, DE, MT, NH and OR.

THRILLS * CHILLS * MYSTERY
from FAWCETT BOOKS

THE GREEN RIPPER by John D. MacDonald	14340	$2.50
MURDER IN THREE ACTS by Agatha Christie	03188	$1.75
NINE O'CLOCK TIDE by Mignon G. Eberhart	04527	$1.95
DEAD LOW TIDE by John D. MacDonald	14166	$1.75
DEATH OF AN EXPERT WITNESS by P. D. James	04301	$1.95
PRELUDE TO TERROR by Helen MacInnes	24034	$2.50
AN UNSUITABLE JOB FOR A WOMAN by P. D. James	00297	$1.75
GIDEON'S SPORT by J. J. Marric	04459	$1.75
THURSDAY THE RABBI WALKED OUT by Harry Kemelman	24070	$2.25
ASSIGNMENT SILVER SCORPION by Edward S. Aarons	14294	$1.95

8400-2